THE PROMISE
OF THE HARVEST

JEAN GRANT

Publishers Since 1798

THOMAS NELSON PUBLISHERS
Nashville • Atlanta • London • Vancouver

Published in Nashville, Tennessee, by Thomas Nelson, Inc., Publishers, and distributed in Canada by Word Communications, Ltd., Richmond, British Columbia, and in the United Kingdom by Word (UK), Ltd., Milton Keynes, England.

Scripture quotations are from the NEW KING JAMES VERSION of the Bible. Copyright © 1979, 1980, 1982, 1990, Thomas Nelson, Inc., Publishers.

Quotes from *Of Mice and Men* are from John Gassner, ed., *Twenty Best Plays of the Modern American Theater* (New York: Crown Publishers, 1939).

Library of Congress Cataloging-in-Publication Data

Grant, Jean.
   p. cm. — (The Salinas Valley saga ; bk. 5)
   ISBN 0-7852-8105-3
   1. Women medical students—California—Fiction.
2. Young women—California—Fiction. I. Title. II. Series:
Grant, Jean. Salinas Valley saga ; bk. 5.
PS3557.R2663P757 1996
813'.54—dc20   95–34692
                                                    CIP

Printed in the United States of America
1 2 3 4 5 6 7 - 02 01 00 99 98 97 96

In the early summer of 1970, several large vegetable growers in the Salinas Valley signed contracts with the powerful, and at that time independent, Teamsters Union. Cesar Chavez, founder of the United Farm Workers, fresh from his victory in organizing the workers in the vineyards of California's Central Valley, announced his next target would be the lettuce growers of the Salinas Valley.

Chavez, a powerfully charismatic leader, led the march of July 31 to August 2 and galvanized the farm labor force.

The valley was polarized; it seemed that everyone was required to take sides in the year-long labor unrest that followed. Names were called; charges were made; incidents of violence occurred from both sides.

The Promise of the Harvest is a work of fiction, set against this background. The businesses mentioned, the events pictured, and the people portrayed—with the exception of Chavez himself—are entirely imaginary, and any resemblance to actual businesses, events, or persons is purely coincidental.

Chapter One

The streets of Salinas were quiet, too quiet for an early Monday morning in July, Holly Stevens reflected as she drove across town toward the hospital. No trucks. No rickety flatbeds laden with lettuce headed for the packing houses. No big refrigerated semis full of crated lettuce on the way to market. Holly's father, who managed one of the largest packing sheds, had been so preoccupied that morning with the Teamsters' strike that he'd scarcely thought to wish her well on the first day at her new job.

Holly slipped her not-so-new Volkswagen bug into a slot in the staff parking lot. She gave her casually flipped strawberry blond hair a quick check in the rearview mirror, smoothed nonexistent wrinkles from her crisp new Size 5 lab coat, took a deep breath, and said a quick prayer for courage as she slipped out of the car.

A cool morning fog promised a typically mild July day in Salinas. Holly sniffed. She'd almost forgotten the faint smell of chocolate from the Nestle plant. It always hovered over the south end of town when the air was still. In a month or so the pervasive smell would be of cabbages and onions, less tempting than the scent from the candy factory but no less familiar.

Holly was glad to be home to stay after four exciting years at the University of California at Davis and a busy year of training in Oakland. But she was nervous, too, about beginning her job as a clinical laboratory technologist. *When I was a student, someone else always checked my results,* she reminded herself, *but now I'm on my own. Doctors will make decisions based on my reports. Sick people will depend on the tests I run.* God, she silently prayed as she walked into the hospital building, *don't let me make any mistakes.*

Tom Tanner, the chief tech, grinned cheerfully as she slipped shyly into the lab. "Hi, Holly, welcome to the snake pit." He gestured to a shelf full of blood collection trays. "Help yourself and check out your supplies. Kathy will take you with her on rounds this morning," he told her.

"Kathy, this is Holly, our new tech. She's fresh out of training. Why don't you take her along to Maternity? That'll break her in a little easy."

"He must like you," Kathy said. Her dark hair fell in a long, fat braid down her back, and she didn't look any older than Holly, but she surveyed her tray and Holly's with a practiced eye. She added a few Band-Aids to hers and a handful of alcohol wipes to Holly's. "A year ago, when I came, he started me in Intensive Care."

"Maybe he just doesn't trust me."

"Nonsense. He wouldn't have hired you if he didn't

trust you," Kathy assured her. Holly wasn't about to tell Kathy that Tom Tanner had hired her because he and her father were American Legion buddies. She followed anxiously as Kathy led the way out of the lab and down a maze of corridors.

"That's Pediatrics." Kathy pointed to her left. A little farther down the hall, she paused. "The nursery." They both peeked in at the babies as Kathy showed Holly where to find isolation gowns and masks. "And don't panic, Holly. You don't have to remember everything at once. We won't send you off on your own for a week or so."

The rounds of the maternity wing were easy; Kathy watched approvingly as Holly collected the routine post-natal blood samples. "Holly's had lots of practice drawing blood," Kathy assured their patients. "She's only new to us."

Back in the laboratory, Tom introduced Holly to an older tech who in turn introduced her to the lab routine. But at lunchtime, Kathy reclaimed her.

"How's it going? Are you totally confused yet?"

Holly nodded. "It's a lot smaller than the hospital lab where I trained," she said, "but there seem to be so many things to do at once. I'm used to running fifty blood counts but not twenty blood counts and a dozen differentials and a half-dozen prothrombin times all at the same time. I like it, though. I can't imagine ever being bored."

"Sometimes . . ." Kathy shrugged. "And sometimes, of course, it's awfully hectic. But in a smaller lab, at least you get to follow individual patients. That's one reason why I took this job. How about you? How did you end up here?"

"I've lived in Salinas most of my life. My mother's a Hanlon, as in McLean-Hanlon Enterprises, and my dad manages one of the packing houses. They both grew up down the valley in Soledad."

"Maybe you know Cici, then." Kathy waved over a short, plump woman who was just leaving the cafeteria line. "She lives in Soledad."

The woman who joined them might have been any age from thirty to fifty. Her coal black hair was drawn back into a bun; her black eyes flashed fire, lighting up her olive complexion; her round, slightly Asian features were cut by a wide smile. *The original happy face,* Holly thought, as she smiled in return.

"This is Holly Stevens, our new tech," Kathy said. "And this is Cici—Felicidad DeLaCruz. Cici's official title is laboratory assistant, but she really runs the place."

"I'm only the dishwasher," Cici demurred, her smile growing even wider.

"Don't let her kid you. She makes media, stocks trays, files reports. If you ever need somebody to hold a screaming kid or you can't find something or you just need a friend, Cici's the one to go to," Kathy explained.

She turned to Cici. "Holly was just telling me she's lived in Salinas most of her life. Her folks are from Soledad. I thought you might already know each other or at least have mutual acquaintances. Her mother was a Hanlon."

Cici smiled knowingly at Holly, and her sparkling eyes seemed to laugh at Kathy's innocence. "As in the Hanlons who live over by the mission?"

Holly nodded. "My grandmother and my Uncle Ted live on the old Fort Romie land."

"We live on the other side of the freeway," Cici explained to Kathy. "What you might call the 'wrong' side." But her voice held no rancor as she continued. "The Hanlons are important people in Soledad."

Kathy wriggled in her chair. Holly tried to make light of the comment. "The Hanlons are just farmers, like everybody else in Soledad, east or west side." She turned to Cici. "Have you lived in the valley long?"

"Oh, yes, since right after the war. My husband, Julio, lived there even before that. We met and were married in the Philippines, and he brought me here as a bride."

There was an uneasy silence. Obviously Kathy had no idea how unlikely it was that the Hanlons, of "McLean-Hanlon," and the DeLaCruzes, from the Philippines, would know each other, Holly thought. "So, Kathy," she asked, forcing a change in the subject, "you're fairly new here, I gather. Married? Engaged?"

"Nope, still looking. How about you?"

"I sort of go with a teacher at Hartnell College, but there's nothing official," Holly told her. "How did you happen to come to Salinas?"

Kathy shrugged. "They were advertising for a tech, and they were willing to hire me."

"But you must have known someone here," Holly queried.

"Not a soul. Actually, that was part of the attraction. My family's kind of scattered—Dad's back east; Mom's down in Orange County." She grinned. "Can you imagine me settling down in Orange County?"

Holly tried not to smile because she could, indeed, picture Kathy quite at home in the affluent suburban enclave. "I'm lucky to have such a close family, I know," she said. "But I envy your nerve, going out on your own like that."

The afternoon passed as quickly as the morning had. The skeleton evening crew arrived at 3:30. Holly was introduced to them but faces blurred; she was thankful for name tags. As she hung her lab coat and turned to leave, she found herself alone for a moment with Cici.

The broad smile was still there as the older woman spoke. "I'm sorry about the awkwardness this noon. I do know of your grandmother and of Dr. and Mrs. Cameron. They'd be your aunt and uncle, wouldn't they? They're good people."

"Thank you. And I hope we'll get to be friends." Holly offered a hand, and Cici squeezed it warmly.

"Ready, Mama?" someone called from the doorway, and Holly turned at the sound of the deep, resonant voice.

"I'll be ready in just a minute," Cici answered. "By the way, Holly, this is my oldest son, Philip. Philip, our new tech, Holly Stevens."

Holly scarcely heard the rest of Cici's introduction—something about Philip's being a teacher at Hartnell; something about his having just come back from Delano. Now Cici was talking about her. "Holly went to Davis, too, and she knows some people at the college."

But Holly wasn't listening. She was staring at Philip DeLaCruz. He was a rather small man, but his presence filled the hallway. His tank top revealed taut muscles, accustomed to harder work than teaching, she saw. His black hair was too long, well down over his collar, though she had to admit it was clean and neatly combed. He wore a disconcerting black beard, setting off a thin, straight nose and prominent cheekbones. Deep laugh lines creased his dark skin. His eyes, like his mother's, were dark, but fiery.

Holly's heart thumped. Philip smiled and stretched out a surprisingly broad, strong hand in greeting. She offered her own, and he took it lightly. "I'm glad to meet you, Holly Stevens," he said. "I hope we'll have a chance to get to know each other."

She felt his intense eyes appraising her. She gulped and hoped he didn't notice. "Yes," she whispered. "I hope so too."

Holly couldn't stop thinking about Philip DeLaCruz as she drove through the small-town congestion of downtown Salinas into the summertime quiet of the college neighborhood. She pulled into the driveway beside the brown-shingled bungalow that had been her home for the past dozen years. *A Filipino, probably Catholic, with long hair and a beard and hands like a dirt farmer's.* He was strikingly handsome, of course, but there was something else, a vague familiarity, that made her uncomfortable.

Cici told me they grow strawberries. It must be a little place if Cici has to do the lab's dirty work to make ends meet. Still, he's teaching at Hartnell, just like Greg, she reminded herself. *And both of my grandfathers—all the Stevenses and Hanlons and McLeans, in fact—started out as dirt farmers.*

But what was he doing in Delano? He could have been working with Chavez. He looks the part. His bearded face and fiery eyes blurred, for just an instant, into another face, a face she had hoped she'd forgotten. *He's not my type at all,* she muttered. But the flame in his eyes still burned into her own, as the timbre of his voice still rang in her ears.

Greg Michaels was waiting on the wide porch that sprawled around two sides of the house. "I just thought I'd drop by on my way home." He kissed her lightly on the cheek. "So, how did the first day go?"

She had only been back for a week, and Greg had been there almost every evening. *I'm glad he's teaching summer school, or he'd be here all day too*, she had found herself thinking more than once. *Now what's the matter with me? I should be thanking God for Greg. He's probably the most eligible bachelor in Salinas. He could date any girl in town; yet he's always been my guy.*

She sighed as she followed him to the porch swing. "Tired, honey?" he asked.

"I guess so," she lied. "There are so many new people to meet and new things to learn."

He sat down next to her, and his arm circled her shoulders possessively. "So chuck the job and marry me."

She edged away. "Greg, I told you I wanted to work for a while. I want to feel useful. I need to prove I can take care of myself. Besides, we've been apart for the better part of two years. Don't you think we should get reacquainted before we make any commitments?"

"I don't have any doubts," he assured her. "But I'm patient. I can wait until you get this career idea out of your system."

His lazy blue eyes smiled at her, and she remembered Philip's penetrating stare. They couldn't have been more opposite: tall, blond, open-featured, casual Greg; small, wiry, dark, intense Philip. *Why are you thinking about*

Philip DeLaCruz? You've barely met the man. You know nothing about him.

"Hey, you seem to be miles away," Greg protested. "I asked you if you wanted to go out to supper Saturday. The head of the Ag. department has invited some of the faculty to a barbecue. Nothing fancy. I'd like you to meet them."

Holly's mother, Ellen Stevens, stepped outside. "Are you staying for supper, Greg?" she interrupted. "It might be a little late. Ron just called to say he's tied up in a meeting, but he should be home around 7:00."

"I guess I'd better not," he answered. "I've got test papers to grade tonight." He glanced at Holly. "About Saturday?"

It sounded terrible. *I'll be on display,* she thought. *Everybody will know everybody else, except me.* But Greg was waiting for her answer. It was important to him. "Oh, sure. I'll go."

Ron Stevens, like most people in Salinas, liked an early supper and a long relaxed evening at home. He hadn't had many of those lately, and he wasn't in the best of moods when he parked his late model Olds next to Holly's old VW in the driveway. But he kissed his wife and hugged his only daughter as he entered the kitchen. "Did Tom get you off to a good start, Holly?" he asked. "I warned him if he gave you a bad time I'd vote against him at the next Legion election."

"Dad, I told you, no favors."

Ron hugged her again. "Have I told you how happy I am to have my second-best girl home again? Of course I expect my friends to help me take care of you."

Holly noticed that her father's bad leg dragged as he

went upstairs to wash up while Ellen and Holly put supper on the table. "He only limps like that when he's exhausted, Mom. It's the strike, isn't it?"

"I don't think he's had a good night's sleep in a month," her mother replied sadly. "He tried so hard to avoid this strike, but he's only an employee himself, really. He wants to do right by the workers, but his first responsibility is to the stockholders."

The little family gathered around the supper table and Ron bowed his head. "And," he added after thanking God for his bounty, "Lord, give me the wisdom to deal justly with both my employer and our employees."

"Dad, why did they strike this time?" Holly asked as they began to eat. "You've been working with the Teamsters Union for years—the drivers, anyhow. Does it matter so much that they want to include the people in the sheds? You always said you wished you could pay them better, but the competition wouldn't let you. If they're in the union, and all the packers have the same contract, won't everybody be better off?"

"I guess so." His drawn expression belied his words. "But somehow it just doesn't feel right."

"You said yourself that the terms aren't that bad."

"I'm not worried about the bottom line, not if we settle soon anyhow." Ron shook his balding head. "But money isn't the real issue. Sure, we might have to raise lettuce prices a little, but then, it's only fair for those people to make a decent living. But . . ."

"Then what? Why don't you just recommend signing? You know they all listen to you."

"The decision isn't mine. And even if it were, including the shed workers in the union contract without an election . . ." He passed a platter of meat loaf to his daughter. "Don't you worry about it, anyhow. You've got enough to think about with your new job and Greg. By the way, has he proposed yet?"

"About every five minutes."

"He's a nice kid, Holly."

"He's good to me, Dad, and he's a good Christian man. I suppose one of these days I'll see how lucky I am and say yes. But I wish he'd give me a little space."

Ellen smiled at her husband and daughter. "If it's right, it will work out in its own time."

If time itself isn't the problem, Holly thought. *We've been a couple for so long we take each other for granted.* "Maybe, for Greg and me, there's already been too much time," she muttered. Her father and mother exchanged worried glances across the table. *They have their doubts too,* she realized.

Chapter Two

*B*y Thursday, Holly was beginning to feel at home in the lab. Kathy, the only other young, single woman, had already made her a confidant. "Have you met Cici's son, Philip, yet?" she gushed over lunch. "Is he ever a hunk."

Holly nodded, trying to be casual as she remembered his lean, taut frame and chiseled features. His ravishing smile only intruded on Holly's thoughts every ten minutes or so as she tried to concentrate on learning the quality control methods in the hematology department's procedures manual that afternoon. Somehow it seemed perfectly natural to find him waiting in the hall as she hung up her lab coat at quitting time.

"Hi," he greeted her. "Holly, isn't it? I'm waiting for my mother," he explained. "I've been using her car."

She stretched for her purse on the shelf overhead, but it slipped out of her grasp. He picked it up and handed it to her. His hair brushed her cheek, and she trembled.

"I hoped I'd run into you," he continued. "I was wondering . . . I know it's short notice, but I wasn't sure until today that I would be free. Do you happen to like gospel music?"

"Love it!" she answered without thinking.

"Then if you're free tomorrow night, would you like to go to the concert at the community theater with me?"

Now she hesitated. He was dressed, again, in jeans and a tank top. Her eyes swept his long hair and dark beard. The shadowy feeling that she'd seen him somewhere before was still there. *Probably at Davis; Cici said he had gone there.* His broad, open smile won out over her doubts. "I'd love to go to the concert with you."

"Till tomorrow, then, about 7:30."

Holly was pleased to see her father's car in the driveway already and to see the smile on her mother's face as she went in the back door. "Hi, Mom." She gestured toward the car. "Is that good news?"

Ellen put a finger to her lips. "They signed early this afternoon, thank God. The shed's reopening in the morning. I sent your father upstairs for a nap."

But Ron was still subdued when he joined his wife and daughter for supper. "Of course I'm glad the strike's over," he told them, "but I'd still feel better if there had been an election."

"But then you would have had to include Chavez and his Mexican farm workers' outfit, wouldn't you?" Holly protested. "Look at what happened in Delano, over the grapes. You know what kind of people are working with him. They're bad news." She thought again of

Philip's long, black hair and faded jeans. *Like Vic. He's too much like Vic.*

"Like Judy's friends?" Ellen sighed. "Have you heard anything from her lately?"

Holly tried not to think about Judy. She was Sam McLean's daughter, and Sam was Ellen's first cousin. The girls had been inseparable buddies from the day the Stevenses had moved back to the valley, when Holly was ten and Judy nine—until last fall. "Nothing since the postcard from Detroit before Easter."

"I thought she went to New York," Ellen interrupted.

"She did, at first. But then they started going around organizing peace marches. Either they lost their jobs with the United Farm Workers or Chavez ran out of money to pay them. They've been living in communes, probably using drugs and sleeping around." Holly's voice was angry, but her eyes filled with tears for her cousin. "She wasn't raised like that any more than I was. Why couldn't she see that Vic and his friends were nothing but trouble?"

"She really hates the war, Holly. Wasn't that what drew her to him to begin with?"

Holly's lip trembled as she thought of the details her parents didn't know. "Lots of people hate the Vietnam War, Mom," she said softly. "But most of us don't take to the streets and burn the flag."

"She took her brother's death awfully hard," Ron commented.

"So did her father," Holly protested. "It was so terribly cruel of Vic to insist to Sam that his only son died for nothing."

14

"It was Sam who forced Judy to choose between them," Ellen reminded her daughter.

"I know, Mom, but Vic practically forced him to it, baiting him every chance he got. If he had really loved Judy, he would have been more sensitive to her father's feelings. You know Judy never wanted to make that choice."

"She did choose, though," Ron insisted. "You can't blame the friends she chose for the mess she's made of her life."

The friends she chose. Holly shuddered. Suddenly the shadowy memory came into focus. *I have seen him before!* "I've got something in my eye," she lied, excusing herself before the tears could force their way under her burning eyelids. Safe in her room she gave way to the grief and the anger and the guilt.

How could I have forgotten? But she had only seen him once and then from the back of the packed dining room at Barrington Hall in Berkeley. *And afterward? Was he in Vic's room later?* She was fairly certain the speaker for the evening had not joined them there. Vic . . . That was the night I introduced Judy to Vic.

Holly had met Vic first, in the laundromat near the little attic studio she shared with Judy. He'd been nice enough, helping her retrieve a jammed quarter from a coin-devouring clothes dryer. "I don't remember seeing you around here before," he'd said, eyeing her approvingly, "and I think I'd remember. Here for summer session or just getting ready for September?"

"Oh, I'm not going to Cal," she'd explained. "I

15

graduated from Davis in June and just started training as a medical technologist."

"Which is . . . ?" He frowned, as if annoyed at the need to ask.

Holly was already used to both the question and the hint of annoyance. She smiled. "Medical technologists are the people who hide in hospital basements and do blood tests, urinalysis, stuff like that."

"Oh, I see. Sounds messy, but I guess it's useful. I didn't realize it took a college education, though."

"Most people don't." She resisted the urge to instruct him on the complexity and importance of the obscure career she'd picked. "Anyhow," she rattled on nervously, "I'm training at a hospital in Oakland, and my cousin and I just moved into an apartment over on Sacramento Street. She's a senior."

She took her first good look at him. He was dark, swarthy even, with a thick black beard, and his long, wavy hair would have been enviable on a girl. Back home in Salinas, maybe even at Davis, they would have bothered her, but in Berkeley, in 1969, neither seemed extraordinary. He looked too old to be a student. "And you?" she asked. "Do you teach?"

"Thanks for the compliment." He laughed, but even then she'd noticed a rough edge to his laughter. "I'm a law student."

The next Saturday morning in front of a Safeway store he handed her a flyer urging her to boycott nonunion grapes, and she actually stopped to read it. "It makes me think," she'd admitted. "I've never really heard much except the growers' side, being from Salinas and all."

"Salinas?" he'd bellowed. "Now there's a great example of worker exploitation. We're having a rally Monday night. You should come and learn what's really going on at these big corporate farms."

"He's right in a way," Holly had explained to Judy. "I should go and hear the other side. Besides, the meeting's at Barrington Hall, where my dad lived when he was at Cal, and I'm curious to see it inside. How about going with me?"

What Holly remembered most about the meeting itself was the noise. She'd gone to learn, to listen to the workers' complaints and hear for herself just what this man, Cesar Chavez, really wanted. But the dining room was packed with shouting kids. The speaker . . . *What makes me think it was Philip DeLaCruz? I never saw him up close.*

But she remembered his voice. It had been compelling even then, though few of the slogan-shouting kids in the room seemed to be listening to his plea that farm labor be granted the same right to organize as other American workers. She knew the argument. *Agriculture's different. Crops are perishable.* But she recalled that at the time his words had made sense too.

It was surprising how vividly she still recalled the evening. She had glanced at Judy once or twice, astonished to see her staring, mesmerized, at Vic. After the meeting, he had invited both of them to a "little discussion group" in his room. But it was Judy's hand he took as he led the way upstairs.

A dozen kids jammed into the room, dropping onto the unmade twin beds. Holly shoved aside a stack of boycott leaflets and perched on a scarred oak desk. She was uncomfortable. Even at Davis the old rules about women in men's rooms, and vice versa, had been dispensed with before Greg had graduated, but, rule or no rule, she'd never been upstairs in his dorm.

If Judy felt equally out of place, it didn't show. She sat cross-legged on the rumpled sheet, giggling, as Vic whispered in her ear. Judy was always falling into and out of love—not at all like Holly, who had been Greg's girl since high school.

Judy went out almost every night that fall. Sometimes it was to a meeting or a rally; sometimes to a party. Holly went to a few of the meetings, but she put in eight hectic hours a day in the hospital lab and had to study several hours every night to pass her state exam the next summer. Besides, the one-sided tirades turned her off.

Soon Judy stopped inviting her to the parties, and Holly was sure she knew why. She confronted her cousin once, just once, about the sickly sweet odor she noticed on Judy's clothing. Judy didn't deny it. "If you're so goody-goody," she'd smirked, "how come you know it's pot anyhow?"

"I did spend four years at Davis, you know." Holly colored.

"Now I know it's true. Everybody really does do it," Judy jeered. "Absolutely everybody."

"But once was enough—too much," Holly insisted. "It's wrong, Judy. You're not in control when you do drugs."

"It's no worse than booze." Judy had smiled, then. "Of course you don't drink, either, do you?" Judy turned out the light and covered her head with her pillow.

At first Holly laughed off her cousin's obsession with

Vic, just as, at first, she laughed off Vic's obsession with his causes—first the United Farm Workers and then the Vietnam War.

"When does he have time to go to class?" she'd asked Judy that day in early October. "Seems like he spends most of his time picketing or demonstrating or setting up rallies. Maybe he has a point about Nam," she reflected. "I know we're trying to protect the people of Southeast Asia from the Communists. And the domino theory makes sense to me. If we let Vietnam fall, what about Thailand and Indonesia and . . . ?"

Judy started to interrupt, but Holly continued. "I know. The war's doing terrible things to the people there. Do they really want our help, at that price?"

"That's my cuz, always seeing three or four sides to every question." Judy shook her long, carrot-red ponytail. "Even my gung-ho brother's not so sure we're doing the right thing."

"But he's still doing his duty, Judy. He's over there fighting because that's where his country sent him. Don't you feel disloyal to him going to these peace demonstrations?"

"No." Judy tied the black band around her arm and started for the door. "I'm working to bring him back home, where he belongs. Maybe you'd feel the same way if your precious Greg weren't safe in the National Guard."

Judy had come back to their apartment late most nights since she'd met Vic. But that night she didn't come home at all. It was the first big Vietnam moratorium march in San Francisco. Some protesters were arrested, and Holly stayed up all night waiting for a phone call.

She had to leave for the hospital early the next morning. Judy was at the apartment when she got home. "Not to worry," she assured Holly. "We just had a little party after the demonstration."

"All night?"

"All night," Judy had told her.

She hadn't even bothered with an excuse. "This isn't the Salinas Valley, Holly. This is the real world. Grow up." A year later, Holly could still see the crooked little half-smile. "So I spent the night with Vic. Why not? We love each other."

The summer sun had set in Salinas, but Holly's thoughts were still in Berkeley. *We were so close before, but Judy wouldn't listen to anyone—not me, her father, or even God.* "The Bible?" she'd scoffed. "It's just a book, like any book, about another man-made religion. It's like Vic says. God is in us. We have to follow the god in ourselves, what we feel."

Vic and Judy were both arrested in November, in San Francisco, along with dozens of other peace demonstrators. Judy's father, Sam McLean, had bailed them both out with a blustering lecture about honor and responsibility. After that, Judy had packed most of her clothes and moved in with Vic, although she still stopped by Holly's apartment to pick up her mail.

"Doesn't it bother you just a little bit," Holly had protested, "picking up a check every month from your father and using it to support Vic and his causes?"

Judy shrugged. "Dad makes his money exploiting migrant workers and captive consumers. Better some of it should get into the right hands, one way or another." After that, she picked up her mail while Holly was at the hospital.

Until the semester break. Right after Christmas, Sam's only son, Bill, had died on a "pacification mission" in a village in the Mekong Delta. Judy had gone home between semesters to be with her father and to grieve with him. She'd taken Vic with her.

"Vic only told him the truth," Judy later insisted as she gathered her last few belongings from Holly's apartment. "Bill should never have been there; he died for nothing. Dad ordered Vic out of the house—and me with him."

"But you're all he has left, Judy. Your mother's gone, and now Bill. Just give him a little time," Holly had pleaded.

"He made it very plain that Vic wasn't welcome, Holly."

"But you don't have to leave school and everything. Your father will come around."

Judy snapped the buckle on the bulging duffel bag. "He's cut off my allowance. We don't have any money. And what's the use anyhow? Why stay here and waste my time just for a piece of paper?"

"You've already put in over three years. It doesn't make sense to quit a semester short of your degree. And Vic's in law school."

"No, he isn't." Judy's cocksureness began to give way. "He flunked out." She picked up the bag. "He's got a job, though," she said defensively. "He's going east to work for the grape boycott."

"You don't have to go with him, Judy. You can move back in here and finish school. Then . . ."

"Vic's my man. I love him, and I'm going with him."

That was the last time Holly had seen Judy. There had been a couple of postcards. That was all. *I should have seen through him sooner.* Holly turned and tossed on her bed. *I never should have introduced them. Oh, God, watch out for her and bring her back to us, and to you.*

I knew she was using pot and suspected worse. I knew she was living with him. Oh, God, I'm sorry, she prayed into her pillow. *I should have tried harder to stop her. But I was afraid if I pressured her, I'd lose her entirely.*

A knock on her bedroom door brought Holly back from her memories. "Are you all right?" her mother asked softly. "You said you had something in your eye, but that was hours ago."

"I'm fine, Mom. I was kind of tired. I lay down for a minute, and I must have dozed off." She heard Ellen's footsteps retreating and fell asleep, exhausted.

Chapter Three

*S*he woke before the alarm went off. Sleep had dulled the hurt but not banished it. *Why was I thinking about Judy?* she questioned for just an instant. Then she remembered she had made a date with Philip. *I could call and make some sort of excuse.* Nonsense, she told herself firmly. *It couldn't have been him I saw in Berkeley. Somebody like that would never be interested in a Christian concert.* She felt warm as she remembered his tender smile. *Philip isn't like Vic. Lots of decent men have long hair and beards.*

"If Greg shows up this afternoon," she warned her mother over breakfast, "please tell him I'm going to be busy tonight. I'm going to that gospel concert with some friends from work."

"How come you're not going with him?" Ellen asked.

Holly laughed. "I suggested it last weekend, and he acted like I wanted to go to a topless bar or something. To most of my generation I'm incredibly square, but then there's Greg. He thinks Christian music has to be a hundred years old and solemn."

"Well, I can't say I really like this new stuff, but I figure I'm just old and stodgy. Or maybe it's my overexposure to your Aunt Marianne and her Salvation Army bands. Anyhow, have a good time. Will you be home for supper?"

"Oh, yes. He . . . they are picking me up about 7:30."

If her mother heard the slip she didn't mention it. Greg called just before the family sat down to supper, and Holly made her own excuses.

"Oh, well, okay," he muttered. "I guess there's nothing really wrong with that stuff. As long as you like it, I'm glad you found some girls to go with." She didn't bother to correct him. "See you tomorrow, though."

"Sure. See you tomorrow."

She hurried upstairs after supper. She pulled a slim, short dress from the closet and rejected it as too dressy. She finally selected a pleated white skirt and a knitted shell in turquoise, to match her eyes.

A glance in her mirror revealed a girlish face—pert, snub nose; a hint of a dimple in her chin. She deftly applied pale lipstick to a mouth she thought of as too small.

She heard the doorbell. "Oops," she mumbled. "I meant to meet him at the door."

If her parents were surprised they didn't show it. She was pleased to see that while he still wore jeans, the tank top had been replaced by a pale blue sport shirt. She forced herself to make the introduction casual. "His mother works at the lab. My mom and dad, Ellen and Ron Stevens."

Philip nodded to Ellen and accepted Ron's offered hand. "Nice to meet you, Mr. and Mrs. Stevens."

By the time the concert ended, the summer fog had blown a chill into the valley. "How about a hamburger and some hot coffee?" he suggested.

Holly wasn't hungry, but somehow she didn't want him to take her home yet. "Sounds good," she agreed. "The music was great, wasn't it?"

"It gives new meaning to 'make a joyful noise,'" he said. "I'm afraid to some it is just noise, but then, when you listen to the lyrics there's a lot of truth there."

"Yes," she agreed. "And I can't help believing God is pleased even if the form isn't traditional."

"He looks on our hearts, and I saw a lot of people with hearts full of praise tonight." Philip pulled into the drive-through lane and ordered their snack.

He chose a well-lighted parking space and offered her one of the hamburgers. "And it's one of the best ways to reach people for the Lord too."

"I agree." She took a bite and studied his face as she ate. "Kids who wouldn't go near a church for anything will go to a good concert and hear the gospel." *I figured he was Catholic,* she reflected, *but he doesn't talk like one.* "Do you go to church?" she asked.

"I do now," he told her. "Mother took me to the Catholic church when I was a kid, but I didn't pay much attention until a year or so ago. I had some Christian friends, and I could see what the Lord meant to them. That's when I was born again."

"I guess I just assumed you were Catholic."

He smiled. "Because I look like one? No, not anymore. I've been going to the Assembly of God here, when I'm home. Mother shakes her head, but I guess she figures it's better than no church at all."

"We're Baptists," Holly said. "I was saved when I was just a little kid." She smiled. "I don't know much about the Assembly of God, but isn't it charismatic—tongues and all that?"

It was his turn to smile. "I suspect you're as dubious as my mother. You'll have to come with me sometime."

They finished the hamburgers and he took her home. Although he didn't mention seeing her again, she was sure he would.

Her mother was still up, even though it was after midnight. "Got interested in a late movie on TV," she lied, unconvincingly.

Holly smiled. "You really didn't need to wait up for me, you know. I'm a big girl now."

"I know, I know," Ellen protested. "Did you have a good time?"

"The concert was pretty good—a little loud, but there was a real message and the crowd seemed moved."

Ellen busied herself with putting away newspapers and turning off lights. She seldom questioned her daughter openly about her private life anymore, but Holly knew she was waiting for answers.

"He's just back in town; he's working on a doctorate from Davis; and he's going to be teaching at Hartnell this fall. I met him the first of the week, and he happened to ask if I'd like to go to the concert." She flashed a smile. "Anything else you want to know?"

"What about Greg?"

"Greg didn't want to go to the concert, Mom. And

we agreed when he graduated from Davis and we knew
we'd be apart for two years that we were free to see other
people." She felt uneasy under her mother's gaze. "So
what if I let him think I was going out with some girls. I
just couldn't see any reason to make a big issue out of it."

"You said his mother worked at the lab. Is he from
around here?"

"His folks have a little farm down around Soledad, as
it happens."

"Oh. I didn't recognize the name. What did you say
it was?"

"DeLaCruz." *I don't have to give her Philip's credentials,*
Holly found herself thinking. But she answered the un-
asked questions anyhow. "They're in strawberries. Mr.
DeLaCruz came here in the 1930s from the Philippines.
He was in the army in World War II, and he married
Cici there and brought her back as a war bride."

"Oh, Filipino. I assumed he was Mexican. Not that it
matters," Ellen hurried to assure Holly. "Catholic?"

"Would you believe Pentecostal?"

"Well, I'm sure there are good Christians in Pentecostal churches and Catholic for that matter."

"Mom." Holly stifled a yawn. "It's past my bedtime.
And I just went to a concert with him. It isn't as if I were
contemplating marriage."

Greg picked her up early Saturday evening. "Did you
enjoy the concert last night?" he asked casually.

"It was pretty good," she told him. "You should have
gone."

"You look like your first week's work agreed with
you," he went on. "That's a cute outfit." He appraised

the tailored green pantsuit that made Holly feel, and look, cooly professional. "You'll make those faculty wives look like something out of last year's Sears catalog."

Holly was uncomfortable as she glanced around the crowded backyard. It was important to Greg that she make a good impression, but she'd always dreaded facing crowds of strangers. Besides, the other teachers in the junior college agriculture department were all older. Holly felt out of place among the faculty wives in their summer print dresses, clustered around the long picnic tables chattering about their children.

Greg rescued her from the gossiping matrons. In each hand he carried a limp paper plate heavy with steak and baked beans. "I got us some supper. Let's go sit down. There's someone I want you to meet. He's an old dormmate from Davis, and he's joining the faculty this fall."

She hadn't seen him come into the yard, but now she noticed the long black hair, conspicuous among his elders' conservative trims. As they approached, he rose and turned. She felt the color rise to her cheeks as she recognized Philip. *He's shaved off the beard*, she noticed, with more than a touch of relief.

"Well, we meet again." He glanced from her to Greg, and back, again, to her, and his ready smile faded. "I guess I didn't connect the name. Greg's told me a lot about you—about his girl, anyhow."

She sat next to Greg across the table from Philip and stared down at her plate, avoiding the hurt in his eyes. "Holly Stevens?" an older faculty member asked, and she looked up, grateful for the distracting question. "You're

Ron's daughter aren't you? Sure good news about the strike, isn't it?"

She nodded. "We're all glad it's over."

"Yes," the older man affirmed. "And the rumor is that most of the big growers and the co-op are talking to the Teamsters too. Maybe we can get this whole thing under control before that Commie, Chavez, knows what's going on."

Philip looked past Holly to the speaker, and she realized his eyes still burned, though the smile was gone. "The growers' co-op?" he inquired. "And the Teamsters?"

"Yup. Looks like we'll get the whole lettuce industry tied up with a real union. Reasonable leadership—people we can talk to, who understand how business really works."

"What about the workers?" Philip's voice was soft, but the question carried the length of the table. "How do you think they feel about the Teamsters representing them?"

"Why should they care?" another teacher asked. "Surely they can understand that the Teamsters can get more for them than they can get for themselves."

"Chavez won't like it," someone down the table muttered.

"Chavez? What's he got to do with it?" the first man insisted. "He's just an opportunist who's picked up a reputation with a bunch of those hippie do-gooders."

"He's a voice of hope for the workers," Philip said firmly. "He and the United Farm Workers offer a way for hopeless, helpless people to help themselves."

Holly squirmed. She hated scenes, and Philip seemed bent on making one.

"The Teamsters can give them a better deal and one within the existing system," another teacher injected. "Chavez's people don't want a union; they want a revolution."

"Maybe, in a way, they do want a revolution," Philip admitted. "But not a Communist one like you're afraid of. They don't want to change the system. They just want access to it, and Chavez has shown them a way."

"Just because he got contracts with a few grape growers doesn't mean he can call the shots here."

Some of the voices were becoming angry.

Holly tried to avoid Philip's face, but everyone else seemed to be watching him as he answered. "The workers love him. The farm laborers in the Salinas Valley don't want the Teamsters; they don't understand the Teamsters. But they trust Cesar Chavez."

The gray heads didn't seem shocked at the audacity of their newest colleague. His voice carried an authority beyond his years and position. They watched and listened. Holly found herself watching with them as Philip concluded. "If the growers drag their workers into a Teamster contract, those workers will call on Chavez. And Chavez will come. And this valley will never be the same."

The faculty party broke up early. "Too bad we had to get into that argument," Greg apologized. "I don't know what Phil was thinking of, sticking up for Cesar Chavez that way. But then, he was always kind of a radical."

"I'm surprised you know him. I don't remember meeting him at Davis." Holly tried to shut Philip's fervent voice out of her mind. "Were you good friends?"

"Not really. We just lived in the same dorm. He graduated and moved out a year ahead of me, though, so you probably never met him. I'm surprised he even remembered my mentioning you."

"I wonder what he's been doing since he graduated," she mused.

"He got a fellowship and went for a doctorate," Greg told her. "He's working on his thesis—something about farm labor. I guess that's how he got in with the United Farm Workers."

"I hope he's wrong."

"I'm sure he is. Everybody knows they're just a bunch of Red, hippie, do-gooders."

Holly remembered her parents' words. "Some of them are, but not all. And the workers really do have a right to organize, don't they?"

Greg's car pulled up in front of the Stevens' house. "Come on, Holly. You know we treat our workers decently here. If they didn't like it, they'd go back to Mexico. Besides, if we gave them everything Chavez wants, the farmers would all go broke. If I didn't know better, I'd think you were on their side."

"I'm not on anyone's side," she insisted. "Maybe I want to be on everyone's side. Nobody wins a strike, especially a farm strike."

"Yeah," he conceded. "Anyhow, there's nothing we can do about it." He walked her to the front door and bent to plant a kiss on her forehead. "I'm more interested in us."

She stood on tiptoe to return the casual caress and remembered how Philip's gaze met hers eye to eye.

Chapter Four

There's Cici," Kathy pointed out as they glanced around the hospital cafeteria, trays in hand. "Shall we sit with her?" She bent close to Holly's ear. "Maybe we can pump her about that handsome son of hers."

Holly hadn't mentioned her Friday date to Kathy. Somehow it seemed too personal to chatter about with her new acquaintance. She followed Kathy silently.

Cici greeted them courteously as they sat down, but she seemed preoccupied with a newspaper. Holly noted it was a Spanish language paper and saw the word *huelga* in one of the headlines. *Strike*, she translated with a shiver.

Kathy ignored the paper in Cici's hands. "Is your son still in town?" she asked.

"Yes." Cici glanced at Holly as she laid the paper aside. "I guess he'll be here the rest of the summer after all."

"You said last week that he was only here for a few

days and wouldn't be back to stay until September, when he would start teaching," Kathy probed.

"Maybe, maybe not," Cici answered curtly. "Plans change." She picked up the paper again.

"I'll bet you're glad to have him home," Kathy persisted.

"Of course." Cici gave up and laid down the paper. "But he's busy, you know, working on his doctoral thesis," she added with a touch of pride. "He is very anxious to finish it this winter."

"I saw him at the Ag. department barbecue Saturday night," Holly told them, still neglecting to mention the Friday night concert. *It's none of Kathy's business*, she told herself. "It turns out he and Greg are old friends."

Kathy nudged her and winked. "Let's fix up a double date," she whispered.

Holly evaded the suggestion. "He seems to be quite an admirer of Cesar Chavez," she commented.

"He's been working with the United Farm Workers for the past two summers, doing research for his thesis," Cici explained. "He's very interested in farm labor organization."

"He thinks there's going to be trouble here, doesn't he?" Holly asked.

Cici nodded. "They don't want it, you know. Most of the workers are afraid for their jobs, but they aren't going to like it if the growers force a Teamster contract down their throats."

"I don't think my mother's family wants any union contract at all," Holly offered. "They've always run the farm their way. They don't take advantage of their help, but they don't want some union telling them what to do."

"McLean-Hanlon has a good reputation," Cici agreed. "But even there . . ." She paused, studying Holly's face. "Holly, so many people have so little hope—some of the Filipinos, most of the Mexicans."

"But you've done well. You own your farm, and you're sending your kids to college," Holly protested. "Doesn't that prove it can be done?"

"Right after the war it was easier," Cici explained. "Julio had his army pay, and he could get a GI loan. But now, for the younger people, there is so little hope. That is what Cesar Chavez offers them—hope."

"But the UFW isn't really a union is it?" Holly asked. "I mean, lots of people say it's more like a political movement. They say Cesar Chavez is really more of a Mexican Martin Luther King Jr. than he is a union organizer."

"Sometimes it's hard to tell the difference," Cici conceded. "Is a struggle for decent working conditions a labor question when the workers are white and speak English but a civil rights issue when they happen to be dark skinned?"

Kathy stifled a yawn. "I thought we already had laws about workers' rights to join unions if they want to. What's all the fuss about?"

"The laws don't include agriculture," Cici told her. "In most industries the UFW could sign up members and force an election, but on the farms it's different."

"It has to be," Holly protested. "The crops are perishable. A car company can wait out a strike; a lettuce grower can't."

"Another thing I don't understand is where the

Teamsters Union comes in," Kathy queried. "I thought they were mostly truck drivers."

"They're crooks, if we believe what the newspapers tell us," Cici commented.

"My father says they offer the growers stability." Holly tried to explain what she couldn't quite understand herself. "They will agree not to strike during the harvest, for instance, and, because their leaders understand how big business works they, well . . ."

"Sounds to me like what you're trying to say is that they speak the same language." Kathy laughed, but neither Holly nor Cici smiled at the lame joke as they headed back to work.

"Pediatrics needs a stat CBC," Tom said as they went into the lab.

"I'll get it," Holly offered, picking up a tray and hurrying down the hall.

The brown-skinned toddler in the crib was chubby but lethargic. He felt feverish, Holly noted, as she picked up the pudgy hand and cleansed a little finger with an alcohol wipe. He didn't try to pull his hand away, even when she pricked the finger with a lancet.

He whimpered weakly as she drew a drop of blood into her pipette and added it to the vial of diluent on her tray. The blood looked pale; it rose too quickly in the tiny glass tube. She repeated the procedure and wrapped a Band-Aid around the finger. She looked at the two vials as she mixed them between her fingers. Even diluted, the fluid should have been a distinct red, but what she saw was a sickly orange-pink.

"Milk baby," the nurse muttered as Holly passed her

desk on the way out. "Why can't those people learn to feed their kids right?"

"Milk baby?" Holly queried. "It does look like his red count is way down." She frowned. "He isn't pale, but then, you couldn't tell, could you?"

She hurried back to the lab and fed the diluted sample into the automated counter. The blood count on the report form it spit out was even lower than she'd expected. She gasped and called the report to the ward.

"We get them all the time," Kathy told her.

"But he's so weak. I'm afraid we got this one too late," Holly worried.

"Don't fret. He'll get some iron shots, and someone will explain to his mother what he needs. They give the kids plenty of milk, you know, but nothing else. They don't think about malnutrition because the babies are so nice and fat. Usually they wean them before the anemia gets that bad, but sometimes . . . Anyhow, he'll be taken care of now."

Cici joined Holly that afternoon as they left the lab. "Philip is using my car again, so he's picking me up in the parking lot," she commented.

Holly realized her heart was thumping again, despite her gloom about the baby. *How silly. Why do I feel like a schoolgirl with a crush on a new teacher?*

He was waiting at the back door. "Hello, Philip," she said, trying to sound casual. "I admired your nerve in standing up to the faculty the other night."

"Somebody has to tell them what's going on," he snapped. "Ready, Mother?"

He was so nice on Friday, Holly thought as she drove

home. *But that was before he realized who I was. What does he think now? That I'm a spy for the growers?*

Greg was on the porch when she got home—again. His lips brushed her cheek as she met him on the steps. "You made a really good impression at the barbecue," he assured her. "Everybody liked you."

"I'm glad they approved. I felt awkward at first, being the only one in pants and all."

"Dean Harding said you were cute."

"I'm not sure 'cute' is the effect I was looking for." She pushed the kitchen door open, and he followed her in. "Hi, Mom."

Ellen turned from the sink where she was peeling potatoes. "Oh, I didn't realize it was that late already. Hi, Greg," she added.

Holly felt the strain in her mother's voice. "What's wrong? More trouble at the packing shed?"

"No, not at the shed." Ellen sighed. "I just got off the phone with your Uncle Ted. The growers' co-op's come to an 'understanding' with the Teamsters to represent their field workers. Bob's after him to do the same thing."

"Bob's nothing but an adding machine with feet," Holly snapped. She'd never been close to her mother's brother Ted, McLean-Hanlon's general manager, or to his son, the corporation's accountant. But Philip's warning echoed in her ears. "I thought they were just talking."

"He said several of the members were panicky. They'd heard Chavez was threatening to take on the lettuce growers, so they forced a vote this afternoon. It will make it very hard for us independents."

"I gather Mr. Hanlon doesn't like the idea of signing with the Teamsters," Greg commented. "Is McLean-Hanlon really big enough to go it alone?"

"Ted feels we can stall for a while. You know how he is, Holly. Sam and Uncle Harry still think we can go on as usual."

Ellen turned to Greg. "You remember my cousin, Sam McLean, don't you? He's field manager, and my Uncle Harry's chairman of the board."

Greg nodded. "My dad knows them both. He says Harry McLean probably knows more about farming than anybody here in the valley. If he's not worried, you shouldn't be."

"As Ted says, a lot of our field hands come back to us year after year, and they know we'll be fair. But Bob insists we'd be safer with the Teamsters, especially with all the big outfits signing."

Greg nodded again. "We need a stable work force. Some of the big corporations have already signed; I think they all will. With the co-op on board, too, the Teamsters can just strike you and force you to go along. You'll probably have to meet their pay scale anyhow, so you might as well have a say in the negotiations."

"But your friend Philip said the field workers wouldn't like being forced into the Teamsters Union," Holly reminded him.

"They're getting a raise." Greg shrugged. "That's all they care about."

On Tuesday, Cesar Chavez announced "economic war against this conspiracy," comparing the growers' action to Pearl Harbor.

And on Tuesday, Holly did two more blood counts on the milk baby. He was still much too quiet. He was in a cool, steamy croup tent, and he was being given oxygen. His breathing was shallow and raspy.

His red blood count had risen a little. *He's had a transfusion*, she deduced. But his white count had skyrocketed. "He has pneumonia," she told Kathy. "He's too weak from the anemia to fight off the infection. He just lies there, staring out of those big brown eyes. He doesn't even have enough strength to cry."

On Wednesday, hundreds of farm workers rallied in Soledad. Chavez spoke for about twenty minutes, and the papers reported that the building rang with shouts of "Viva Chavez."

And on Wednesday, there was no lab order for the baby. Holly stopped at the pediatrics ward. "Yes," the nurse told her flatly. "We lost him during the night. It was just too late."

"Why didn't they bring him in sooner?" she asked Cici when she got back to the lab. But she already knew the answer. "Don't they understand that we'll take care of them even if they don't have the money?"

"Pride," Cici answered. "Or ignorance, if they don't realize how sick the children are. Or fear, if they're here illegally and think we'll report them to Immigration. They really need a clinic of their own."

On Thursday, the workers began to march. They came east, from the strawberry fields near Aptos on the coast. They came south, from the onion and garlic fields of Gilroy. They came west, from Hollister, where the tomatoes were beginning to ripen. And they came north, from Greenfield, through Soledad. The four groups would meet in Salinas on Sunday.

Holly saw Philip only once, as he dropped Cici off one morning. He didn't speak. *What do I care anyhow?* she tried to persuade herself. *He's just another self-appointed crusader, like Vic.*

Greg took Holly to see *True Grit* on Saturday night. "The Duke hasn't lost his touch, has he?" he commented as they munched hamburgers at McDonald's after the movie. "That was more of a downer than most John Wayne epics."

"Mmmm," Holly grunted. "Oh, I'm sorry. I'm afraid I wasn't paying a lot of attention."

"To the movie? Or to me?"

"Both, I guess," she admitted. "What do you think is going to happen?"

"About what?"

"Tomorrow, with this workers' march?"

"Oh, I hoped you meant between us."

"Greg, please, you promised to give me some time."

"Okay, okay. Why are you worried about tomorrow?"

"You know why. In Soledad on Wednesday, Chavez's people drove all over town after the rally waving signs and yelling and throwing garbage on lawns."

"Did they bother any of your folks?" He seemed concerned, at last.

"Nooo. Not really. But they threw some rotten tomatoes at Bob's neighbors. And Grandma Carrie's nearly ninety, and so frail. Suppose they call a strike and start picketing like in Delano. They beat up people there."

"There's not that many of them, really. The TV people like to blow those things out of proportion. It makes a better story."

"I hope you're right." Ugly scenes from TV screens crowded into her mind, scenes out of the past. She fought against the memory of Judy's face suddenly appearing in a San Francisco mob, screaming as the police dragged her off. "Greg, mobs have a habit of getting out of hand."

"Yeah, some of those people might be looking for trouble—not our own workers of course. They don't want a strike anyhow. But I hear Chavez has picked up a following of hippies and Reds. You know the type. Some of them would probably love to start a riot."

"I know all too well," Holly told him. "Chavez talks nonviolence, but suppose somebody does something that looks suspicious, like at Kent State, and somebody else gets scared and starts shooting."

"You don't know what really happened at Kent. Just maybe the National Guard was in the right. If somebody started throwing rocks at you, wouldn't you fight back?"

"With a gun? Okay, maybe you're right. We weren't there. But everybody says some of Chavez's followers are pretty wild."

"Might be a good idea to stick close to home tomorrow, just in case, but I'm sure the police are well prepared," he assured her.

"I just hope nobody gets hurt, on either side."

"If that so-called union had just kept its nose out of it, there wouldn't be any rally. If things get out of hand and some of them get hurt, that's tough."

"What about your friend, Philip?" she asked.

"Phil? What's he got to do with it?"

"He's working with Chavez, isn't he?"

Greg seemed surprised. "Hey, he's got some leftist ideas, but Chavez is just part of his doctoral research."

"I hope you're right."

"Holly, what's going on with you and Phil? He hasn't made a pass at you or anything, has he?"

"I . . . No, nothing." *Well, you couldn't call a date for a gospel concert making a pass, could you?* "I know his mother from the lab, and he seems nice. That's all. And . . ." She laughed, a short, nervous, laugh. "He's awfully good looking. It would be a shame for such a handsome face to get mashed in by some policeman's billy club."

Chapter Five

*I*sn't Greg coming over this afternoon?" Ron asked as Holly began stacking the Sunday dinner dishes. "I can help your mother with those."

"No, Dad. He was nervous about having his car on the street this close to the college with the rally and all."

"So that's why you cleaned out the garage yesterday," Ellen said to her husband. "And I thought it was just my nagging," she added with a nervous chuckle.

"Now don't fuss. It just seemed like a good time to get it done. Now that Holly's home, she shouldn't have to park in the driveway all the time."

"And there might be trouble, mightn't there?"

"I don't think so," Ron insisted. "But any time you get several hundred people together . . ."

"Ron, do you think you'll be a target because of the contract at the shed?" Ellen asked.

"That's preposterous," he insisted. "And there's no reason to expect a riot, either. I talked to a few people who were actually in Soledad last week, and nobody got hurt, absolutely nobody. There wasn't even any property damage to speak of."

"But you still put both cars in the garage," Ellen reminded him.

"And now I'm going to read the Sunday paper." Ron leaned back in his easy chair and propped his feet on the ottoman. "Home and Garden." He tossed a section to his wife. "Still want the funnies first?" he asked his daughter.

"I think I'll go out on the porch." Holly took the local news section of the paper. "Traffic seems to be picking up."

"Maybe you should stay inside," Ellen protested.

"Don't be silly, Mom. I'm just going to sit on my own front porch. Besides, isn't it better to know what's happening than sit in here and worry?"

Ellen looked to Ron for support, but he only shrugged. "If I didn't think I'd be too conspicuous, I'd go over to that rally myself. Nobody's going to do anything to Holly on her own front porch."

The tree-shaded street was lined with large, well-kept homes. Neatly trimmed hedges separated wide, weed-free green lawns. On a normal Sunday afternoon neighbors would have chatted as they tended their rose bushes. And, though none of them were farmers, the talk would often have been about crops and the difficulty of hiring good farm labor and lettuce prices.

The garage doors were usually wide open on Sunday afternoon, too, for ready access to power mowers and bicycles. Teenaged boys generally washed cars in driveways. Today, Holly suddenly realized, the cars were all behind closed garage doors, just as the people were shut in behind the doors of their placid middle-class homes.

Cars began to be parked on the peaceful street—mostly old cars, dented station wagons, rusting pickup trucks. Families with black hair and olive skin, all dressed in their Sunday best, climbed out of them. The men and boys wore clean jeans and loose white shirts; the women wore flowered cotton skirts and white blouses. Holly smiled at the little girls in stiffly starched, ruffled dresses, with bows in their jet black hair. *Are these the people I'm supposed to be afraid of?*

The children skipped along the sidewalks, laughing and pointing at the brightly blooming perennial borders. Some of them carelessly twirled flags—red, white, and blue American flags; green, white, and red Mexican flags; red flags with black eagles, which Holly had seen before only on television. The parents walked purposefully toward the nearby junior college athletic field where the United Farm Workers' rally was to be held.

The noise from the neighboring streets focused in the direction of the college, just a couple of blocks away. At first Holly heard, mostly, the shout of "Viva Chavez." Then there was relative quiet—a voice, using the PA system no doubt, but out of her hearing, and an occasional shout of "Cesar, Sì; Teamsters, No." But then it became a chant, a roar, almost. *"Huelga! Huelga!"*

Strike! Holly shivered. Philip had been right. War was coming to the Salinas Valley. The chanting ended, and the dark-skinned people began returning to their old cars.

Her father came to the door. "Holly, maybe you should come inside."

She shook her head, and he came out and sat on the swing with her. "I've been listening to the radio. Chavez called a strike, and he's threatening a lettuce boycott too. Just what I was afraid of."

"You were afraid of it, and Uncle Ted's afraid of it. But Philip is afraid of it too. So why is it happening Dad?"

"Philip?" Her father studied her face. "Just where does this Philip fit in?"

"He's just someone I met." She swung for a few minutes. Her father was obviously waiting. "His mother works at the lab. He's going to be teaching at Hartnell this fall."

"I know. But I gather he's involved in some way with Chavez. And he seems to have made quite an impression on you," Ron prodded.

"Not really," she lied. "But he's been working on a doctorate in farm labor relations, and he said if the co-op signed a contract with the Teamsters covering the field workers, the United Farm Workers would fight it." She could hear the words, in Philip's calm, measured voice. "Dad, Uncle Ted and Bob both said the workers would be better off under the new contracts. So why are they so angry?"

"Maybe they don't like being told what to do any more than your Uncle Harry or your mother's cousin, Sam, do." His voice had a bitter edge. "What right do we have to tell them what union to join?"

"But is the UFW really a union? Greg and most of the other people I've talked to think it's run by Communists."

"I've seen some long-haired hippie types around, including young DeLaCruz," Ron conceded dryly. "Does that necessarily mean what they're supporting is wrong? I certainly don't want to see a strike in the fields, but . . ."

"Dad, I know you didn't want to sign with the Teamsters even in the packing shed. It's not just the Hoffa scandal, is it?"

"There should have been an election, an honest, open election, with every choice on the ballot—Teamsters, UFW, no union. The workers should have a right to choose who's going to represent them."

"That seems fair." She paused, thoughtfully. "Dad, that's so utterly reasonable. Why didn't it happen?"

"You know what a 'sweetheart contract' is, don't you?" She nodded. "Well, we got one whale of a 'sweetheart contract.' We're telling ourselves, and everybody else, that everybody won, but that's not true. My stockholders won; the Teamsters Union won; everybody else lost."

Most of the cars had left the street, and neighbors began to emerge and gather in tight little knots, talking over the clipped hedges. One last dark-skinned family walked toward one last old Ford.

Two teenagers led, talking excitedly. An old man with leathery skin walked proudly behind them, head held high. A woman, younger, walked beside him, head bowed almost as if in prayer. Holly didn't recognize her at first, but she knew instantly the lithe young man who strode on the other side of the old man. So that must be Philip's father, Julio.

The DeLaCruzes had been to the rally. She started down the sidewalk toward them. Cici didn't look up, but Holly was sure Philip had seen her. He quickened his steps and hurried his parents toward the car parked at the end of the block.

"Holly." She jumped as her mother called to her. "Holly, are you going to evening service with us?"

After church, Greg invited himself over for supper. Ellen set a place for him next to Holly in the breakfast nook. "We don't have to be fancy and use the dining room, do we?"

"I guess not," Holly agreed, as Greg took his place in the cozy window seat.

Ron thanked God for their food and for his family and prayed for both farmers and workers. "Lord, give us the wisdom to know what is just and the strength to do it."

"You don't really think this strike will go anywhere, do you?" Greg asked, as Ellen passed a platter of cold chicken to him. "Surely most of the workers—the real workers, not that bunch of troublemakers from Delano— would rather work under a Teamster contract than go on strike. They need their jobs."

"I don't know, Greg," Ron answered. "Maybe they've finally gotten fed up."

"Surely you don't think they're justified, Mr. Stevens."

"Have you ever been in the fields or in the labor camps? I know your dad's a grower, but have you ever really looked at his workers' housing or talked to his field hands?"

Greg shifted uneasily on the bench next to Holly. "Of course I have. And don't tell me about the farms where the migrants live in dug-out caves without latrines or clean water. You know that's just made up for the bleeding hearts. Nobody does that."

"Your father doesn't. Thank God not many growers do, but there are some. I've seen it. And would you want to live in what your father does provide?"

"Well, no, but they aren't used to any better. In Mexico they live in a lot worse."

"But they've come here for better," Holly interrupted.

"And they have better," Greg insisted.

"Better than in Mexico," Ron admitted. "But is that enough?"

"So the new contracts call for better pay, better housing, even health insurance for the people who work steadily. What more do they want?" Greg pressed.

"Maybe what they want is respect."

Holly said it, but her father picked up on her words. "Maybe they want to be asked what they want instead of being told what they are going to get."

"But a strike will hurt them even more than it will us," Ellen reproached. "Even if we lose this year's crop, we have savings to fall back on. They don't. Without their weekly pay, how will they eat or pay their rent?"

"Which is precisely why this strike won't last more than a week or two," Greg insisted.

"I hope and pray you're right," Ellen agreed.

God, Holly found herself praying silently, *let it come to a just resolution.* She remembered Julio DeLaCruz's pride, Cici's concern, and, most of all, Philip's determination. *And please don't let anyone get hurt.*

Chapter Six

The strike came. UFW members picketed at fields owned by co-op members. They carried cardboard signs and red and black UFW flags. And where they marched down the dusty farm roads, the long rows of lettuce along the fences went unpicked.

It was almost a game that first week. UFW scouts drove the back lanes; when they saw workers in a field, they called in their loyal members or a handful of the students who were spending their summer vacation working for the cause. When the pickets came, the workers stopped picking. Sometimes they joined the pickets, but often they just moved on to another field, often part of the same large farm.

Holly saw Philip once or twice at the hospital. Though her heart still pounded at the sight of him, and though she knew his fiery eyes never failed to sweep over her, he scarcely spoke to her.

Greg continued to turn up at the house almost every

day. During the first weekend of the lettuce strike, he had asked if she'd like to go to a movie, and Holly had suggested a play instead. "Hartnell really has a good summer repertory theater, and they're doing *Of Mice and Men* Sunday."

The houselights dimmed in the small college theater. A single spotlight focused on George and Lenny crouched at one corner of the bare stage.

George turned his head away from the tiny object that dangled from two fingers of his outstretched hand. A dead mouse.

Lenny hitched up the baggy trousers that sagged on his bulky frame. ". . . just a dead mouse. I didn't kill it. Honest. I found it. I found it dead."

Greg sat beside Holly with one arm casually about her shoulder. It felt, well, normal, *like it belongs there*, she thought. *But what would it be like if it were Philip's arm?* She shivered just a little at the uninvited thought.

The summer rep player was a good Lenny. Holly actually forgot, for a while, about the strike, as she found herself caught up in the play. Lenny wheedled childishly, "I don't know why I can't keep it. It ain't nobody's mouse. I didn't steal it. I found it layin' right beside the road. I wasn't doin' nothing bad with it. Just stroking it."

But Holly was jolted rudely from her appreciation of the performance as crude laughter broke out from scattered spots in the audience. Her instant amazement was pushed aside by a sickening shock. They were laughing, actually laughing, at the pathetic child-mind tyrannized by its own powerful man-body.

Steinbeck's tragic tale continued. Lenny, whose chief

pleasure in life came from touching soft things, could not keep his hands from crushing his pets even as he stroked them. And George, his reluctant guardian, was impotent to keep Lenny out of trouble.

The laughter continued too. As the tragedy unfolded on the stage, Holly felt an even deeper tragedy. She was horrified that a sizeable part of the audience found Lenny's helplessness and George's hopelessness funny.

Now and then Holly glanced at Greg. He hadn't joined the laughter. In fact, he seemed more bored than anything else.

When they stepped out into the cool mist at intermission Greg commented on her moodiness. "You're not enjoying the play much, are you? I think they're doing a pretty good job."

"It's not the play, Greg. The performance is fine, but . . ." *Maybe he didn't notice. Maybe I'm the only one who's bothered.* "But I don't think Steinbeck's meant to be enjoyed," she said, "especially *Of Mice and Men.*"

"Yeah, I guess you're right. It's not really entertainment."

"Then why are they laughing?"

"Laughing? Oh, that." A grin spread across Greg's face. "Well, if you didn't already know the story, you could think some of it is pretty funny."

Holly shook her head. "I don't see how."

"Oh, Holly, you take things too seriously. It's just a play."

The laughter decreased as the wrenching events of the second act sobered most of the audience. But even as Lenny, in uncomprehending panic, broke the neck of the equally unwitting trollop, even as her limp, soft body fell to the stage floor, Holly heard a few snickers.

Greg suggested a pizza on the way home, and Holly shrugged assent. "It really got to you, didn't it?" he prodded as he set a mug of root beer in front of her. "I remind you, you were the one who wanted to see this play. I knew Steinbeck was morbid."

"It wasn't so much the play. I expected it to be a downer, but, Greg, they kept laughing."

"Is that still bothering you? Lots of people don't read plays before they go to see them. They didn't know about the end."

"They knew he was handicapped. They knew Lenny was severely retarded, and that made him an object of ridicule. How can people be so insensitive?"

"Ah, come on, Holly. A few people laughed at a guy in baggy pants who wanted to pet a dead mouse. When you look at it that way it really is a little funny."

She saw the smile before he had time to force it from his face. "How can you look at it that way?"

"I don't. Really I don't," he protested. "I didn't laugh. But I don't think it's such a big deal when a few people who haven't had a college course in American literature miss the point. Holly, it's only a play."

"Is it? Are you sure those same clods wouldn't laugh at a real-life Lenny?"

"Even if they would, you can't make it your problem. People are people." Greg picked up a slice of pizza and flicked his tongue at a trailing string of melted cheese. "Better get your share of the pizza before I eat the whole thing."

"Go ahead and eat it. I'm sorry, but I'm just not hungry."

Cheese dribbled down his chin. "Now that's funny," she told him, forcing a smile.

He caught the hot yellow ribbon with a napkin. He picked up a slice and held it to her lips, and she bit off the drooping tip. *He's really a good person,* she reminded herself, *and I think he really loves me. But . . .*

Holly nibbled at a slice of the pizza. Then she realized Greg was waving at someone across the crowded pizza parlor and was startled to see Philip and Kathy coming toward them. Kathy was giggling, as usual. Philip, Holly realized, held back, obviously suggesting they take another table. But Kathy dragged him forward.

"This guy says we shouldn't bother you two," she gushed as she sat down and waved Philip into the seat opposite. "But we were invited after all." She winked at Greg. "Holly and I are old friends already, and you two fellows are, too, so I say we should all get acquainted." She paused for breath. "Did you two go to the play over at the college?"

"Yes," Greg said. "Pretty good for a small town, don't you think?"

"I loved it."

Does Kathy love everything? Holly wondered. She looked at Philip, who seemed intent on the second pizza, which had just been served. "It's a heartbreaking tragedy, isn't it?" she asked softly. "A tragedy, in the Greek sense, with no resolution."

He nodded.

"Greg and I were just talking about the audience reaction." Holly didn't want to reopen the quarrel with

Greg, but he and Kathy seemed engrossed in their own impressions of the play. She directed her soft words only to Philip. "I don't see how anyone could laugh."

"If you can't cry and you won't fight, maybe there's no other choice but to laugh," Philip answered soberly.

His eyes met hers just for an instant, flashed in the dim light, and dropped to his plate.

Kathy and Greg chattered on, seeming not to notice the silence of their dates, until the remaining pizza was cold.

"Now that's an odd pair," Greg commented as he drove Holly home.

"How so?"

"Well, Kathy's so lively, full of fun. And Phil's such a sober guy, all wound up in 'causes' and stuff. Even before he got religion I never thought of him as the life of the party."

"What have you got against his religion?"

"Nothing, I guess," Greg edged. "But he does take it awfully seriously."

"Don't you?"

"Sure I do, Holly, but, well, you know the type."

"But I don't," Holly protested. "I know he's a Christian, but so am I. So are you."

"But I don't go around claiming my political opinions are God's or acting like I'm his personal representative on earth. You don't know Phil that well of course, but he can be pretty irritating sometimes, when he takes off on how God 'demands' justice for the poor and all that."

Holly squirmed. "Maybe he does."

"Who does what?"

"God, demand justice," she mused.

"For Pete's sake. When did you turn into an activist?"

"I haven't." She bridled at the term she associated with shouting and picket signs and police making arrests. "But if you really believe something is right, morally, in accordance with God's law, don't you have an obligation to speak out?"

"If you are in a position to do something, of course. But I can't believe God expects me to tilt at every windmill I see. That's crazy."

"I guess that's true, but . . ." *Judy,* she thought. *What Judy's done, running off with Vic, breaking God's law in the name of freedom, that's crazy.* But Philip DeLaCruz, she knew, wasn't crazy.

Chapter Seven

The next week there was picketing at one of the McLean-Hanlon properties. "I thank God," Holly told Cici as they walked to the parking lot one afternoon, "nobody's been hurt."

Cici nodded agreement. Philip was waiting, again, and Holly managed a glib, "We must stop meeting like this."

His smile was obviously forced. "I'm looking for a car of my own, so Mother won't have to share."

I shouldn't care, she told herself. *Nothing could come of it anyhow. Still, we were so close the night of the concert,* her heart whispered. Then Holly realized there was someone else in Cici's car, a girl.

The door opened, and a tall, thin young woman in faded jeans with stringy, carrot-red hair trailing over her shoulders, jumped out and ran toward them. "Holly!" she squealed.

"Judy? Judy!" The girls embraced. "When did you get back? How do you know Philip?" Holly paused for breath, and turned to Cici. "This is my cousin, Judy McLean." She hesitated, turning to her cousin. "Are you home to stay?"

Philip stood awkwardly, holding the car door open. "Judy's helping the pickets," he muttered to his mother. "I offered her a lift back to Soledad. Judy . . ." His voice rose. "We have to go. I have a meeting tonight."

"Oh, pooh." Judy grasped Holly's hand in one of hers and waved the other toward Philip. "Go ahead. I'm going to spend the evening with my favorite cousin." She turned to Holly. "Phil said you were back in town. All finished with school?"

Philip was still waiting. "Go ahead. Holly'll take me back to camp later," Judy told him.

Holly headed her car toward home, but Judy protested. "Can we just drive around and talk by ourselves? I've missed you—even your lectures. Honest."

"But Mom would be delighted to see you. The last we heard you were in Detroit." *She hasn't mentioned Vic. How do I ask her if . . . ?* "Sam hasn't said anything about your being home," she added.

Judy toyed with a lank strand of hair. "I just came back this week, and my father doesn't know I'm here. Or care, I'm sure."

"That's not true. Sure, he was upset about your getting involved in all those peace demonstrations, especially after Bill . . ."

"Why couldn't he understand? I know he lost a son, but I lost a brother too. If we'd had our way, Bill wouldn't have been in Nam. He'd still be alive."

"Sam's had some time to heal, and you're his only

daughter. You're all he has left. I know he still loves you very much."

Judy shook her head. "When I left last winter, he made it very clear I needn't bother to come back."

"But you have." *With Philip DeLaCruz,* Holly puzzled. "If you're not here to make peace with your father, why are you here?"

"I'm helping the workers."

"I see," Holly said flatly.

"You can just pull over and let me out here if you want to," Judy suggested, "if you don't want to fraternize with the enemy."

"Don't be silly. Besides, I'm not sure who the enemy is."

"So I was right. I told Phil not to write you off. 'Deep down,' I told him, 'Holly's got the right instincts.'"

"Why in the world were you talking to Philip about me?" Holly queried.

"As a matter of fact, he asked me if we were related, and I told him your mother and my father were first cousins," Judy explained. "What's going on with you two, anyhow? He said he just happened to meet you through his mother, but I got this feeling . . ."

"We met; we went out once; but that's all."

"Too bad. He's such a hunk!"

"I thought looks weren't important to you," Holly teased.

"Looks like his? Besides, he's real, inside."

That's what she said about Vic too, Holly recalled. "Have you known Philip long?" she asked.

"Just met him this morning, on the picket patrol," Judy replied.

Holly hoped her relief didn't show.

"You did know he was working with Chavez, didn't you?" Judy asked.

"We hadn't really talked about it. I knew Philip admired him, but I understood he was involved mostly because of his doctoral thesis. I didn't realize he was actually picketing." Holly pulled the car into a hamburger stand. "I have to call Mom and tell her I'll be late," she explained. "Want anything?"

"No, thanks."

Holly took a good look at her cousin. "You look awfully thin. Sure you don't want a cheeseburger and a shake?" Judy shook her head. "I'm going to have something," Holly told her. "You could keep me company."

"Well, okay, just to keep you company, but I'm really not hungry."

Holly drove to a small park, and they sat on a bench with their snack. Judy nibbled absently. *She really isn't hungry*, Holly thought. *But she looks like she hasn't had a square meal since she left Berkeley last winter.*

"So," Holly prodded gently, "where have you been and what have you been doing? I got your postcards from New York and Detroit."

"I went back to work for the UFW, on the boycott. And we won." She laid the hamburger aside half eaten. "We'll win here, too, you know."

"If you call that winning. Can't you see? Everybody loses in a strike, your own family, and the workers too."

"But it's the principle, Holly. Those people have a right to make their own choices. Your own father—I used to think Ron Stevens was a nice enough guy, until he signed that sweetheart deal with the Teamsters. How could he do that with a clear conscience?"

Holly's eyes filled as she thought of her father's struggle. "He didn't want to. But he's just an employee too. He works for the stockholders and the board of directors."

"Stockholders and boards of directors," Judy snorted. "The only language they understand is profit, and the only way they will ever give the workers their rights is by economic force. Strikes. Boycotts. We've just got to beat those monstrous conglomerates to their knees."

Her voice rose, shrill, strident, so unlike Philip's firm, quiet tones. Yet the words weren't that different, Holly realized. "Judy, don't make this a war between us. Can we just change the subject?"

"Okay." Judy's voice softened. "So how do you happen to be dating Philip? What happened between you and Greg?"

"Nothing." Holly smiled. "You might say that's the problem. Nothing ever happens."

"I always assumed you'd do the establishment thing— get married, have a couple of kids, live happily ever after."

"I thought so, too, for a long time, but now I'm not so sure." Holly's words surprised her. "We're still seeing each other. He still talks about getting married, even, but . . ."

"Philip?"

"No," Holly answered a little too quickly. She paused, pondering. "Judy, I met Philip less than a month ago. I haven't seen him more than half a dozen times. We only had one real date. And he's hardly my type." She forced a chuckle. "Can you imagine sweet, square little Holly Stevens and a guy who works for Cesar Chavez? Anyhow, he's been barely civil ever since," she admitted reluctantly.

"Well, he's sure interested. He asked a lot of questions when he found out you were my cousin," Judy said. "And *you* can hardly say his name without choking up."

"It's so silly. Philip and I are so different. I'm surprised he asked you about me. He seems to be angry about something." Holly wiped her fingers and put the napkin back in the hamburger bag. "Maybe it's just the strike and being on opposite sides. But he turned so cold after that one date. He was almost rude at the barbecue."

"What barbecue?"

"The Hartnell Agriculture Faculty barbecue. I went with Greg, but we met . . ."

"So that's it!" Judy shrieked. "That's why he made that crack about engaged girls. Because he saw you with Greg. He got the idea you and Greg were engaged."

"But we're not," Holly insisted. "Did you tell him we were?"

"All I told him was that you and Greg had gone together forever, and I supposed it was possible. But I told him I couldn't imagine you, of all people, dating anyone else if you were engaged to Greg."

"Here I thought he'd turned against me because of the strike," Holly groaned. "It's my own fault, though, hanging on to Greg when I've known for months that I wasn't really in love with him," she confessed. "Everyone thought of us as a twosome, Greg included. I should have broken it off long ago, but I don't know how to tell him. I hate to hurt him."

"Putting it off won't make it any easier on him." Judy drew idle circles in the sand with her toe. "And I'm giving you fair warning," she teased. "If you don't make a play for Philip, I might."

"What about Vic?" Holly seized the opening, hoping

against hope that Judy would tell her she was through with him.

"You had to ask, didn't you? No, Holly, he didn't run out on me. He . . ." She picked at her rough, unkempt fingernails. "He had to stay in Michigan for a while. But we're still together," she insisted. "So you see love doesn't depend on some legal document or some words recited in front of a preacher after all. It would be fun to go out with Philip, though."

Holly's heart was heavy as she drove her cousin to the shabby little cottage on the east edge of Soledad. Judy was staying there with several other young people who had taken time out from college to support the strikers. "You're welcome to stay with us," Holly offered as she surveyed the broken-down porch crammed with rolled-up sleeping bags.

"I can't make pleasant conversation with your folks like nothing is happening," Judy insisted.

Driving home, Holly tried to suppress her excitement. *It's just Greg. Philip does like me, but he thinks I'm Greg's girl.* The evening fog was beginning to drift up the river and over the town. *Just when did it end?* she wondered. But there hadn't been a specific time, just a drifting apart. *Maybe it never really ended because it never really began*, she realized. Certainly she had never felt for Greg anything like the urgent, persistent, unbidden desire that Philip aroused in her.

Careful, Holly, she warned herself. *Don't get caught up in this crazy sixties confusion between love and sex. Look at Judy. She still thinks she's in love with Vic even after the way he's used her.*

But Holly knew what real love was. She had seen it between her mother and father. She had seen it between Aunt Marianne and her husband, Paul. She could even remember seeing it when she was just a little girl, before Grandpa Matt Hanlon had died, between him and Grandma Carrie.

I'm not sure about Philip, she insisted to herself, struggling to quiet her pounding pulse and cool her flushed cheeks. *I'm not sure about Philip, but I'm not in love with Greg. And I have to tell him so, soon.*

"You're so quiet tonight, Holly," her mother commented as the family sat on the porch enjoying the evening breeze. "Are you troubled about Judy?"

"Some, Mom. She's terribly thin. I know she hasn't been eating right. And she's so edgy. She can't sit still a minute."

"She always was high strung," Ellen reminded her daughter.

"I'm surprised she's turned up here after that awful row with Sam last winter," Ron commented.

"I tried to talk her into calling him, Dad. You don't really think he meant what he said, do you?"

"At the time, yes. It's hard to understand a daughter demonstrating against a war your son's been killed in. And that boyfriend of hers . . ."

"You know it broke his heart when she ran off with Vic," Ellen said. "But I gather that's over."

"I'm not sure," Holly replied. "She said he had to stay in Michigan for a while, but I'm sure she was hiding something."

"She needs Sam as much as he needs her. If she can just swallow her pride, I know he'd forgive her."

"I'm not sure she's ready to ask for forgiveness, but I'll see her again. I'll try to get her to talk to him."

They rocked for a few minutes before Holly broke the silence. "Are Uncle Ted, Uncle Harry, and Sam any closer to an agreement about the union?"

Ellen shook her head. "It's still a three-way standoff. Sam's dead set against any union at all; Harry thinks we can work out something with the UFW; and Bob's just about persuaded Ted that the best business decision is to sign with the Teamsters."

"Uncle Ted has the most voting power, with his stock and Grandma Carrie's," Holly said.

"But not a majority. That's really what makes it so messy," Ron explained. "None of them has a majority."

Ellen spoke again. "Ted's asked me to come down on Sunday afternoon for a meeting—he's invited Marianne and Liz too."

"But you, Aunt Liz, and Aunt Marianne don't actually own any stock," Holly puzzled. "Why does he want to talk to you?"

"He said he doesn't really think he should vote Mother's stock on something this important—and Mother insists her half of Dad's stock is really only in trust for us girls. So she refuses to make a decision without talking to us."

"What do you think they should do?"

"I honestly don't know. I admit my sympathies are with the workers, and they seem to want the UFW. But of course I don't have the problems some of the others do."

"Problems?" Holly asked.

"Some of them really need the income from the farm, or they will within a few years. It's the only livelihood Uncle Harry, Sam, Ted, and Bob have. There's Aunt Adele, and Uncle Tim's widow, Nancy, and Sam's sister, Beth—they each own ten percent, and they have their rights. And Mother hasn't any other income either."

Holly knew her grandmother's share of the farm would pass to her three daughters when she died.

"We won't need the money," Ellen went on, "but Liz and her husband are getting up to retirement age. They never saved that much, putting all the kids through college and everything. And Marianne and Paul spent all their lives in China. Now they live on a pittance of a Salvation Army pension. So we have to be realistic. We can't risk losing everything because of some guilt complex, as Bob puts it, about being better off than somebody else."

"Is it just a guilt complex, though, or is it simple justice?"

"Justice, maybe," Ron interrupted, limping heavily as he started upstairs to bed. "But simple it's not."

Holly had been almost grateful when the talk shifted from her moodiness to the ever-present labor troubles. But as she headed toward her bedroom, she recalled again the talk with Judy about Greg. *We're going to the beach tomorrow,* she thought. *I have to tell him then. I have to, before he's hurt even more. And . . .* She tried to reject the thought as somehow unworthy. *And while there is still a chance for me and Philip.*

Chapter Eight

*I*t's a good thing you didn't plan on going to Carmel until this afternoon," Ellen said as Holly came into the kitchen the next morning. "It's still foggy."

Holly nodded absently. "Greg said he'd pick me up around two o'clock. I'm sure it will be sunny by then."

"Are you going to pack a picnic?"

"No, I don't think I'll bother, Mom. We can pick up something if . . ." She watched her mother, elbow deep in flour, kneading dough. "Isn't it a lot of bother to bake bread?"

Ellen laughed. "Sure, but you know how much your father loves it. He always says it wouldn't be Saturday without the smell of bread in the oven."

"You love him very much, don't you?"

Ellen stopped kneading and stared at her daughter. "He's my life—a part of me, just as I am part of him. But what brought on a question like that? Holly, is there something special about your date with Greg today?"

Holly nodded.

"Are you going to tell him you'll marry him?" There was excitement in her voice. Holly could imagine her mother planning dresses and flower arrangements and a reception.

"No, Mom." She could read her mother's disappointment. "I know Greg's a wonderful man, but I just don't love him, not that way."

Ellen nodded. "I guess I suspected it."

"But you're disappointed. You wanted me to marry him, didn't you?"

"Yes, I did," Ellen admitted. "But I'm glad you've made the decision that's right for you. I guess Greg's always reminded me of your father, and I remember how difficult it was for us, at first, how long it took for me to find my way to him. I hoped you'd find the same happiness with Greg that I've found with your father."

"You always loved Dad, though, just as he always loved you. You just had to get your priorities straight."

Ellen chuckled. "That's a good way to put it. You and Greg have always been a twosome, just like we were, but without the complications. You had everything in common, including your faith. It always seemed God intended you to be together."

"You knew, though, before you married Dad, that that was God's plan for you. How did you know? It wasn't just because you were both Christians and had a lot in common, was it?"

Ellen had gone back to kneading her bread dough, and Holly probed further, wanting her mother's affirmation of what she already knew. "You don't make home-made bread every Saturday for a man because he's your best friend. You married Dad because you wanted him, wanted to be with him, couldn't imagine life without him. Isn't that right?"

Ellen patted the springy dough into the waiting pan. "Being best friends is a very good thing. But it's not enough for a happy marriage. I'm glad, or at least I will be when I get used to the idea, that you found that out in time."

Holly hugged her mother. "I knew you'd understand. Now," she sighed, "how do I make Greg understand?"

It was sunny in Salinas when they left, and they chased the retreating fog over the oak-studded Santa Lucia Mountains and down to the startlingly dark, sparklingly bright blue of Monterey Bay. They drove south through Carmel and along the awesome Big Sur coast. The beaches were crowded, of course, but Greg kept driving south until he found an unoccupied turnout overlooking the shoreline.

White surf dashed headlong against granite boulders. The roar carried up the cliff and exploded in their ears. A lone cypress hugged the bluff, leaning into a sheltering cleft.

"There's a way down," Greg told her, opening the car door. "I found it a year ago last spring, when I was over here exploring by myself."

She followed him down, planting her feet in his footholds; accepting his proffered hand in the steepest places.

"It'll be easier going back up," he promised, as he offered her a rocky seat.

"That wasn't so bad," she assured him. "And it is lovely." *Too lovely*, she thought, *for what I have to do.*

"Holly." She was startled by the unaccustomed intensity of his voice. "This place has been special to me for a long time."

"It's beautiful. It's like the whole Big Sur packed into this one little tiny cove."

"And the wonder of it is that we have it all to ourselves." Greg sat cross-legged in front of her as she perched on a boulder overlooking the surf-pounded rocks. "I wanted to share this place with you, just as I want to share my life with you."

For a moment she almost wondered if she had made the right decision. Greg would always be good to her. She watched the waves drift in, one by one, from far out to sea, just a ripple at first, a lacy white edge, then breaking into millions of white diamond bubbles, sparkling for an instant, and disappearing. Sunlight glistened on the wet black rock, and she recalled the fire in Philip's black eyes.

Sunlight glistened on something in Greg's open hand, too, she suddenly realized. She hadn't really been listening, but now, as she saw the ring, she heard his words. He was asking her once again to make their engagement official.

"Greg." She hadn't really meant to shout, but she had, perhaps to make herself heard against the incessant surf and his incessant question. "Greg, can't you see? It just isn't right—us."

Her words shocked him. "But . . ."

"I'm sorry. I should have told you this a long time ago—a year ago, at least."

"Holly, I don't understand. You said you wanted some time, but . . ."

"Everyone expected us to get married. I guess I expected it, too, but I can't get married just because it's expected."

"Is there someone else? Someone you met in Oakland or something?"

"No. It isn't that simple. It's just . . ." She looked at Greg's eyes, realized they were watering, and resisted the impulse to pet him, as she might a puppy.

"Then you just need more time. That's all right. Sure, I'd like to make things official. I'd like you to wear my ring and everything, but if you need more time . . ."

"No, Greg. I don't need more time," she said, a little too sharply. "I just don't love you—not the way I need to love the man I marry."

He started to protest, but something in her voice must have convinced him that she meant what she said. He stood, offered his hand again, and helped her scramble up the steep bank to the roadway.

He silently drove the familiar miles back, along the blue bay and through the golden hills. As they headed into the valley green with unpicked crops, he spoke once more. "It was a good dream, Holly. But I guess it's no good if it's only my dream. It has to be yours too."

"I'm sorry. It isn't your fault. It's just that it wasn't meant to be."

He sighed, a long sigh, *as if he were letting go*, Holly realized.

"I hope you find your dream."

"You're home early," her father commented, turning off the power mower as Holly got out of Greg's car. Ellen, who'd been clipping faded blossoms from the rose bushes, looked up, laid down the shears, and came toward her daughter. Greg, who had not gotten out of the car, pulled away from the curb.

Ellen's eyes asked the question, and Holly answered. "Yes, I told him," she said, suddenly very sad for the part of her life she had put behind her. "It wasn't easy, but it's over."

"Your mother told me," Ron said gently. "Are you okay?"

"I guess, Dad. I'm sorry it wasn't to be, but I'm sure about my decision."

They walked into the kitchen, and Ellen poured lemonade from the pitcher she kept full all summer.

Holly sat next to her father in the bay window, and he took her hand. "I always liked Greg, Holly, but these past few weeks I've wondered. If you're sure—no, if you're not sure, then you've done the right thing."

"Thanks. I guess that was it. I finally admitted to myself that I wasn't sure, and how could I let him go on expecting me to marry him when . . . ?"

They drank their lemonade in silence. Holly half expected one of them to mention Philip. *What would I say if they did?* she wondered. *The truth. I don't know if I'm in love with Philip, and I certainly have no inkling that he's in love with me. We scarcely know each other. But,* she had to admit to herself, *if I felt with Greg what I feel when I'm with Philip, I would have accepted his ring this afternoon, wouldn't I?*

Holly picked up the empty glasses and stepped to the sink to rinse them. Her mother broke the silence. "Holly, I have to go down to Soledad tomorrow afternoon. Why don't you go with me?"

"Why, Mom? You said Grandma Carrie wanted to talk to you, Liz, and Marianne. I gathered the cousins weren't included."

"We don't actually have any votes, either," Ellen reminded her. "But Liz's boys are coming. And we respect your opinions. In fact, it was Marianne who suggested you come."

"She did?" Holly was well aware of the semi-secret bond between her mother and the woman she called her aunt. Holly had been told several years earlier after hearing whispers of ancient gossip, how Marianne had been raped when she was fifteen years old and had borne a baby girl. Grandma Carrie and Grandpa Matt Hanlon had adopted the little girl they named Ellen and raised her as their own. "How come she wants me there?"

"I mentioned that you'd made friends with a Filipino who worked with Chavez, and Marianne thought you might have a different viewpoint to offer." She picked up a dish towel and began drying the glasses Holly had washed. "Confidentially, I think she's looking for an ally."

Chapter Nine

Holly had been too preoccupied with her own future the past few days to keep up with the developments in the fields. Now, as they drove south, her mother brought her up to date.

"So the Teamsters have declared a closed shop in the co-op members' fields, and now they're striking the big outfits that haven't signed yet."

"But the UFW's picketing us. What a mess."

"Actually, they're picketing the co-op too. They're on strike against us because we haven't signed at all, but they're picketing the co-op on the grounds that they had no right to sign with the Teamsters."

"Then it's a jurisdictional strike," Holly said. "I thought that was illegal."

"There's supposed to be a court order coming," Ellen explained.

"How would that affect us, though?"

"It wouldn't, directly. If a union wants to picket our

fields, it can. Of course it can't use force to keep out anyone who wants to work. But . . ."

Ellen looked past her daughter to the ripening fields. "I really do feel sorry for them," she continued. "They need those jobs, but it must be terribly hard to go out and work when your friends are calling you a traitor."

"And when, maybe, you even think of yourself that way," Holly mused. "Mom, they need their weekly pay to feed their kids, but they want their kids to have more than enough to eat. They want them to have a future. That's what the UFW means to them—hope."

Mother and daughter drove on, and Holly looked at the fields that stretched across the valley. The Gavilan Mountains on the east and the Santa Lucias on the west flanked the twisting course of the wide but shallow bed of the Salinas River, with its narrow trickle of muddy water.

It was Sunday, so there would have been few pickers even without the strike. Most of the farmers were irrigating. Pipes longer than football fields stood on wheels taller than basketball players. And long sprays of water arched from the pipes, making rainbows as they fell back to the black soil with its neat corduroy furrows.

The crisp pale green of the lettuce was the most common. Interspersed with it were the bright emerald carrot-top patches and the dark olive of the broccoli. Holly's mind added another green, the one that held them all together. *Money. That's what it's all about, really. Money.*

The willow-lined lane was as familiar as the street she lived on in Salinas. It led, just as surely, home. Since she was a little girl she'd always started craning her neck as soon as they turned off U.S. 101, where the marker pointed the way to the ruins of the old Soledad Mission. There was a museum at the mission site now, and they were trying to raise funds to reconstruct the old adobe walls that had tumbled in earthquakes and crumbled in a hundred years of rain and wind.

Just past the state historic site, Holly could see the peaked gables of the Hanlon farmhouse, amid its circle of willows. The original part, the two central downstairs rooms and Grandma Carrie's kitchen lean-to, were more than seventy years old. So was the idle windmill that still stood next to the house.

Aunt Liz's shiny Plymouth station wagon already sat in the driveway between Uncle Paul's dusty old Ford Falcon and Uncle Ted's new Chevy El Camino. "Looks like they're waiting for us," Ellen said.

"Sam and Uncle Harry aren't coming, I gather."

"No. This isn't an official McLean-Hanlon meeting. And don't say anything, but I sort of hope Bob will stay out of it too. He has every right to try to influence the way his father votes his twenty percent, but this meeting is about Mother's twenty percent."

Marianne met them on the porch. She was tall and slender. Her hair, once flame red, was gray now and pulled severely back in a bun, but her turquoise blue eyes, the eyes she had passed down to Holly, still sparkled with joy. "I'm glad your mother brought you along," she whispered to Holly as she led them into the old-fashioned parlor.

Liz Hendricks, the middle Hanlon sister, sat on an overstuffed couch flanked by her two sons. Her carefully coiffed blue-white hair and stylish navy blue pants suit seemed out of place in the small room overcrowded with photos and keepsakes of two generations of Hanlon off-spring.

Ted had taken his father's old chair opposite his mother. Holly and Ellen brought dining room chairs in for themselves and sat so that they, too, could face Carrie Hanlon.

Holly could scarcely believe Grandma Carrie would be ninety in the fall. She sat bolt upright in the easy chair, hands folded in her lap, reading glasses on a ribbon around her neck. She surveyed the circle and smiled with satisfaction at her children and grandchildren.

Holly thought of the missing grandchildren. Carrie could be proud of them, too—Marianne's three young-est, scattered all over the world, Salvation Army officers all, following in their parents' missionary footsteps; Liz's four girls, all married and settled down; Ted's son, Bob, heir-apparent to the management of the family farm.

They waited for Carrie to speak. "Well, you all know why we're here," she declared. "McLean-Hanlon Enter-prises has a very difficult decision to make. Always, be-fore, I've trusted Ted to vote my shares, but there is so much at stake this time. You three will inherit my stock before very long, so I want you to share in this decision."

She turned to her son. "Ted, would you just tell us, in plain English please, what our choices are?"

Ted did as he was asked, without, Holly acknowl-edged, embellishments or opinions.

"We've done fine without a union up to now," Liz offered when he had finished. "Won't all this strike stuff fall apart by itself in a week or so if we just stand firm?"

"Maybe," Ted said. "But meanwhile we're losing the lettuce crop."

"I don't think it will blow over this time," Ellen said. Holly was surprised by her mother's firm tone. "Feelings are very strong, and the workers have something they've never had before—a leader they believe in."

"Well, we can't afford a long strike, so why don't we do what the bigger farms are doing—head them off by signing with the Teamsters?" Liz said. "You did say the terms they'd offered the co-op were reasonable, didn't you, Ted?"

"For now, yes," he agreed reluctantly. "But who knows what they'll want next year?"

"That goes for that Mexican, too, only more so," one of Holly's cousins countered.

"'That Mexican.'" Holly hadn't meant to say anything, but the ugly slur roused her anger. "First of all, Cesar Chavez is not a Mexican. He's a native-born American citizen. Second, neither he nor the people he represents are stupid. They know they won't gain anything by putting us growers out of business."

"Then why are they stopping our harvest?" Carrie spoke softly, without anger. "Your mother tells me you know some of them. Can you tell us what the newspapers aren't saying?"

"I don't know that much, Grandma Carrie," Holly admitted. "I've talked to a couple of people who are involved with the UFW, but . . ."

"Aren't we here to decide what's best for the company, Mother?" Liz interrupted.

"Yes, but I think what Holly can tell us may help us to know what that is. Go on, Holly," Carrie insisted.

"Well, Philip, the man I know, is working on a doctorate from Davis, and his thesis is on farm labor relations. I guess that makes him an authority, but I really don't know him very well."

She tried to ignore Grandma Carrie's questioning smile as she continued. "Philip is sure the workers will stick with the strike this time. Chavez has enough financial support to provide strike relief for the people who are out of work. And the AFL-CIO has recognized the UFW, so aren't they as legitimate a union as the Teamsters?"

"Heaven knows I don't like the idea of a Teamster contract." Liz grimaced. "That Hoffa! In jail! But then, look at the kind of people who are supporting Chavez. Communists, even, and all those long-haired hippies and peace-niks."

"Why don't you tell us how you feel, Marianne?" Carrie asked.

"Liz, you won't like it," Marianne warned. "We have a chance to make a real difference. We have the opportunity to give some struggling people a hand up, and that's what I've been doing most of my life. I honestly can't believe we'll lose money by letting our workers organize and improve their working conditions. In the long run, I am sure God will reward us with employees who are as interested in our business success as we are, because as we prosper, they prosper."

Carrie smiled. "And you, Ellen. What do you think?"

"I know what Ron went through over the Teamster contract at the shed," she said thoughtfully. "It looks good, on the surface. The workers got a raise, and the shed got a 'no strike during harvest' guarantee. But, because the workers weren't given a choice, Ron didn't feel right about it, and neither do I. I'm sorry, Liz. I can't defend it on the grounds of profit; I don't think it's right to force people into a union they don't want."

Liz nodded glumly. "I suppose you're right."

Carrie spoke again. "I gather we agree that we Hanlon women, at least, do not want to do business with the Teamsters." Ted shifted uneasily as his mother continued. "Ellen, you want us to agree to an election, don't you, and to go along with the results."

It was Ellen's turn to nod. "And, Marianne," Carrie continued, "you think those results will favor the UFW, but you would abide by another decision."

"Certainly, Mother." She looked at her brother. "Assuming the election was strictly aboveboard, of course."

"Then, Ted, you have my decision."

"It isn't what the others want, Mama," Ted warned her. "Uncle Harry will go along, I guess. He's always been a dirt farmer himself at heart. But Sam will never agree to a union contract of any kind. He's determined to 'hold on to our rights as owners.'"

"Sam has only ten percent of the vote, Ted. How about the others?" Ellen inquired.

He ticked them off quickly. "Beth has ten percent; she'll almost certainly go along with Sam. Nancy, as Tim's widow, has ten percent; she wants her income, and Bob says she agrees with him that the Teamsters would be best from a fiscal viewpoint. Adele has another ten percent; she listens a lot to Harry, and to you, too, Marianne."

Carrie had been counting. "Harry, Adele, and I own half the stock."

"And Sam, Beth, Nancy, and I own the other half," Ted reminded her. "I understand how you feel. But the

80

farm is a big business, and the major income for some of us."

"Ted," Ellen protested. "You know Sam and Beth are voting with their emotions. They just hate unions."

"Aren't you and Marianne doing the same thing?"

"Ted, we have a strike in progress in our fields for the first time in our lives, and if it isn't settled within the next week or two we stand to lose a lot of money," Liz protested. "It seems to me that most everyone involved is more concerned, pro or con, about Cesar Chavez and his United Farm Workers than about the bottom line. How about you? You're the general manager, and you seem to have the swing vote. So, what are you going to do?"

The room was silent. Holly was proud of the women who had given her life. *They, at least, are willing to do the right thing. But what about Uncle Ted?*

"I just don't know. Mother, you do understand, don't you? I have to do what I think is best for the company. That's my responsibility as general manager. The co-op thinks it's best to go with the Teamsters, but obviously many of the McLean-Hanlon stockholders don't want to do that. Most of the conglomerates are still holding out against both unions, but they can afford a strike a lot more easily than we can. I just don't trust Chavez," he concluded.

He stood and walked slowly toward the door. "I wonder what Dad would do," he said as he walked out of the room.

"The one thing his father would do," Carrie said quietly with just a hint of regret, "is make a decision." Her hands were still folded in her lap. "But first, he would pray over it. Shall we follow his example?"

Liz excused herself as soon as her mother's prayer ended. "It's a long drive back to Walnut Creek," she reminded them.

"And it has been a long day for me," Carrie told her daughters and grandchildren. "I'm afraid I need a little nap."

Marianne walked to the car with Ellen and Holly. "How are things going with you and Greg?" she asked.

"Actually, there isn't anything between me and Greg, Aunt Marianne. He's a swell guy, but, well, we drifted apart, I guess. So it's officially over, as of yesterday."

Marianne didn't seem surprised. "Both your mother and I found our loves after losing them for a time. Maybe that will happen with you and Greg too." Her eyes twinkled, and the familiar chuckle crept into her voice. "Or maybe not. Should I ask who this Philip is?"

"No," Holly whispered as she hugged the older woman. "Not yet, anyhow."

Chapter Ten

Holly fell easily into the lab routine. *Only a month,* she reflected, as she fed a mid-morning batch of blood counts through the automated counter. *With so much happening in the valley, not to mention in my life, it's a miracle I've been able to concentrate on my job at all.*

The machine spit out a printed report, and she gave it a practiced glance. An outpatient's red cell count was very low, and she quickly ran it again. No milk baby this time; the patient was an adult, and the numbers didn't indicate iron deficiency.

"Kathy," she called. "Have you looked at the smear on Mrs. Jones?"

Kathy flicked through the glass slides on a rack beside her, chose one, and placed it under her microscope. "Wow!" she exclaimed, moving to one side so Holly could look.

The red blood cells on the smear were as pale as the baby's had been, but grotesquely large, as she had expected. She reached for a phone, called Mrs. Jones's doctor with the report, and turned back to Kathy. "Those are the kind I like, where I really feel useful. Most of the interesting stuff is such bad news—leukemia or something. But this looks like a nice, simple, pernicious anemia; something that can be licked. And it looks like we found it in time."

Kathy nodded, and they went back to their work.

It was nearly lunchtime when Kathy received what was obviously a personal phone call. She eyed Holly curiously as she responded in monosyllables. "No, I didn't. Sure, why not?"

She hung up and turned to Holly. "That was Greg, asking me for a date. Just when did you two break up?"

That was quick for someone who's supposed to be heartbroken, Holly thought. "Oh, it had been coming for quite a while. Our relationship obviously wasn't going anywhere. We made it official over the weekend."

"You know, I didn't say anything, but I got the feeling when we ran into you at the pizza place that things weren't going too well."

"Mmmm." Holly finished signing a stack of reports. "So, are you going out with him?"

"Well, if you're sure it's over between you two . . . He seems nice, and . . ."

"He is nice, Kathy. Really he is. But I sort of thought you had your sights set on Philip DeLaCruz."

Kathy shrugged. "Phil's awfully good looking, but we don't really have anything in common, you know." She looked around, *for Cici,* Holly suspected, as Kathy continued in a whisper. "I mean, him being Filipino and so religious and all."

"So religious?" Holly queried.

"Yeah. One date and he starts telling me how important Jesus is to him and how he wants to be a missionary or something. It's okay to go to church and all, but you don't have to get carried away about it."

A missionary? Funny he didn't say anything about that to me, Holly pondered. She waited for Cici to leave for lunch, and then followed, hoping to catch her alone.

Cici sat with two other techs, and Holly joined them. *Well, I couldn't very well walk up to her and announce that I'd broken up with Greg, anyhow, could I?* she thought. *I'll just have to wait for the right opening. Besides, this is a small town. Philip will find out fairly soon one way or another.*

The others were talking about the strike. "We hope there will be an agreement soon between the United Farm Workers and the Teamsters," Cici was saying. "The Catholic bishops have formed a committee to mediate."

"Would that mean one or the other would pull out?" one of the women asked.

"Probably," Cici answered. "The workers do not trust the Teamsters, but most of them do trust their church."

"I hear Chavez is pretty religious, but would the Catholic Church officially take his side?"

"The bishops are mediating, not taking sides," Cici pointed out. "As it is now, the growers are playing one union against the other."

"Interesting as all this is, I think we'd better get back to work," one of the other techs said.

Their two companions left, and Holly moved closer

to Cici. "I know this labor trouble is terribly important," she sighed, "but I do wish the workers could just vote and get it over with."

"Don't we all?" Holly was startled by Cici's ready concurrence. "I only wish it were that simple."

The two women turned to their lunch trays. "Not to change the subject," Cici offered, breaking the uncomfortable silence, "but Kathy tells me you've broken your engagement."

"Engagement? What gave you, or her, the idea I was engaged?"

"I thought you'd said you weren't, when you first started working here, but then someone told me you were. Then Kathy mentioned this morning that you'd broken up with your boyfriend."

"I did break up with Greg, Cici. He had asked me to marry him, but, well, he just wasn't the man I wanted to spend the rest of my life with." Holly remembered Judy's words. *Where did Philip get the idea I was engaged to Greg?* "Cici, I never told Greg I would marry him." *And please, Cici,* she added silently, *be sure to tell Philip that.*

On Thursday, the Teamster-UFW pact was announced, declaring packing shed workers within Teamster jurisdiction and field workers under that of the UFW.

Judy called to gloat. "We won," she assured Holly, but her voice seemed slurred.

"You may have beaten off the Teamsters," Holly warned, "but you haven't won yet."

"What choice do you all have?" Judy insisted. "The workers are solidly behind us. We'll have pickets on every farm by next week, and you'll sign or you can watch the lettuce rot in the fields," she shrieked.

Holly held the receiver away from her ear. "Don't shout at me, Judy. You might be surprised to hear it, but a lot of the family is on your side."

"Who? Oh, Marianne, I suppose. But not Ted, and not Dad."

"Well, maybe not your father, but several of us."

"Does Phil know that?" Judy asked.

"We haven't really discussed it. But, Judy, doesn't almost everybody want the same thing Chavez wants, an honest election?"

"Why haven't you told Philip that?"

"Because I haven't seen that much of him, Judy. In fact, I don't think I've seen Philip since the day you got back."

"And your other problem? Have you broken off with Greg?"

"As a matter of fact, I have. And I guess I have you to thank for making me face up to it. I told him last Saturday that I wasn't going to marry him, ever, and it would be better if we quit seeing each other."

Holly could hear raucous laughter in the background. "Sounds like you're having a victory celebration," she commented to her cousin.

"Yeah."

Holly hesitated, but the question forced itself out. "Is Philip there?"

Judy laughed. "Him! Holly, honey, Philip doesn't come to this kind of party. Didn't you know? He's a saint, like Cesar." Judy's voice faded out as she held the receiver away to speak to someone else in the noisy room.

"Holly, I really didn't call just to gloat," Judy continued. "I called to ask you to help us, to help the union."

"Help? Didn't you say you won? I think most of the growers will agree to elections now, and . . ."

"Oh, I don't mean with the strike. I mean with the clinic. Hasn't Marianne told you about it yet?"

"What has Aunt Marianne got to do with this?"

"Oops." Judy turned away from the phone again, and Holly thought she heard someone offer her a joint. *I've got to try to get her away from that,* she told herself as Judy came back on the line.

"Sorry. I guess I got ahead of myself," her cousin explained. "Marianne and Paul are helping the UFW set up a clinic for its members, and we thought you might help."

"I hadn't heard anything about it." Holly remembered the toddler who died, and Cici's words about a clinic of their own. "I'll talk to Marianne about it, and if I can do anything, I will."

Cici must have told Philip about me and Greg by now, Holly told herself, as she rocked in the porch swing the following Saturday evening. *Surely he'll call soon.* But he'd had all week, and he hadn't called yet. *Maybe I was wrong.* Holly reminded herself that he had, after all, dated Kathy at least once. *Maybe he wasn't as attracted to me as I thought.* She recalled his chill stare that night at the barbecue, and his distant coolness at the pizza parlor after the play. She jumped as she heard the phone ring inside the house.

She could hear her mother chatting. *It isn't Philip, then.* Ellen called from the doorway. "It's Marianne, Holly. She'd like to talk to you."

"I wasn't sure I should ask you," Marianne explained. "I didn't want to make you feel obligated. But there are several hundred farm workers with no health insurance and very little money. The union has rented a place in Soledad for a clinic and has a little equipment. Paul and I have volunteered to work a few hours a day."

"I really would like to help," Holly assured her. "I've seen what can happen." She told Marianne about the baby. "But I haven't had much experience."

"You can do most of what we need, though. Blood counts, urinalysis, throat cultures for the kids, blood sugars for our diabetics, things like that. Paul has a license to practice medicine in California, even though he's officially retired, so there are no legal problems."

"Well, if you don't have anyone better qualified, I'll try," Holly conceded. She hesitated. "Marianne, there's something else I'd like to talk to you about. How much have you seen of Judy since she got back?"

"Not a whole lot. We've talked three or four times, but just for a few minutes. I do wish she'd try to reconcile with her father."

"So do I. But there's more than that. The way she acts sometimes concerns me. I think some of the kids in that house are using drugs."

Marianne's sigh confirmed Holly's fears. "I've got to find a way to spend more time with her," Holly continued. "Judy and I were really close when we were kids, when you and Paul were still in Taiwan. But then she

89

got into some bad company at Cal, and . . . Anyhow, I have to do something to help her."

Holly heard Marianne's infectious little chuckle. "You might have more opportunity if you were working with us at the clinic."

"That's blackmail." Holly's laugh joined Marianne's. *You'd have more chance to see Philip too,* a tiny voice whispered inside her. "I don't have much time. I work from 7:00 to 3:30."

"I know, but we're going to be open from 1:00 to 5:00. If you could dash down here a couple of times a week and work for a couple of hours, you could run the samples we collect and read our cultures. It really would be a big help."

Chapter Eleven

The building the union had rented was a shabby little cottage on the wrong side of the freeway in Soledad. Since the clinic had just opened that afternoon, Holly was surprised to see a half-dozen cars parked on the baked adobe that might have once been a front lawn.

She went inside and was delighted to see Judy sitting behind a scratched steel desk filling out forms for a brown-skinned woman who was trying to quiet a crying baby. Her cousin looked up, obviously pleased. "Holly! Are we glad to see you! Paul's up to his eyeballs in patients, and Marianne's helping him. I think they put your stuff in what used to be the kitchen." She waved toward a closed door.

Holly entered and glanced around the dingy old kitchen. It had been scrubbed clean, but the linoleum floor was scarred, the sink was chipped, and the vinyl that covered the countertops was peeling. The paint on the cabinet doors looked fresh, but she could see that the latest coat covered layers of chipped enamel.

A tiny refrigerator stood in one corner. She looked inside and was surprised to find neatly wrapped packages of commercially prepared culture plates, a few vials of antibiotic sensitivity disks, and a box of reagents for prothrombin time testing.

On the bottom shelf were a few paper cups covered with clear plastic. She smiled. *Marianne knew the urine specimens must be kept cool,* she thought. *But I sure hope we don't get inspected before we can get a second refrigerator.*

Holly was checking the thermometer in the little incubator she'd found next to the sink when Marianne came in. "I know it's not what you're used to, Holly, but it's a lot better than we had in China."

"Actually, I'm surprised at how well you've done," Holly told her. "The incubator's a little too warm right now, and I haven't calibrated the centrifuge. Oh, and lab regulations require separate refrigerators for specimens and reagents. But the microscope looks like a good one."

"You just tell me what you need, and I'll pass the word along. Chavez has contacts you wouldn't believe— money's scarce, but he always knows somebody who knows somebody who can donate what he's looking for."

Holly's "couple of hours" stretched into late evening that first week as she learned to make do. "In a way it's what I used to dream about when I first thought I'd like to be a med tech," she told Judy over supper on Thursday. "It's exciting to actually see the patient and then hand my results to Paul, talking to him about treatments, seeing the patient get well. I love being part of a team."

She told Judy, too, about the baby she couldn't forget. "They'll come here before it's too late. They aren't afraid, here."

Judy was crying, Holly realized. The baby's needless death was tragic, but her cousin's flushed face and rapid breathing were overreaction even so. "Judy, are you feeling all right."

"Sure. Why wouldn't I be?" Judy insisted.

If I confront her with my suspicions I'll only frighten her off, Holly told herself. "You know you can come to me if anything's wrong, don't you? You will let me help?"

"Of course I would, but I'm okay, honest." She picked up her fork, and Holly realized her hand was trembling. "I'm just fine," she insisted.

On Friday afternoon, when Holly arrived at the clinic, the makeshift waiting room was crowded. During the first few days, she'd seen mostly women and children and an occasional older man. But today there were several young men. They huddled together in one corner and spoke in Spanish too rapid for Holly to decipher. Their voices were angry.

The knot unraveled, and she saw Philip at its center. He saw her in the same instant. The other young men drifted off, still muttering, as he walked toward her. "I'd like to thank you for helping out here," he said. "It's good of you and your aunt and uncle to give your time to our members."

"It's really nothing." Could she have forgotten, so soon, his brooding smile and flashing eyes, and how they made the blood throb at her temples? "I'm enjoying the experience," she told him with forced calm. "But why are all these people here? Is there a problem with the clinic?"

"Not with the clinic, Holly. I gather you haven't heard the bad news about the co-op yet."

She shook her head, and he told her, his soft voice as

full of rage as the louder ones of his friends had been. "They've announced that they will honor their 'understanding' with the Teamsters. And the *Teamsters* . . . ," he spat out the word, "most nobly offered to honor the contract as well."

"But the pact with the UFW?"

"It appears the pact wasn't worth the newsprint it took to report it." He stared at her. "It's so unfair."

"Of course it is," she agreed.

"I didn't mean the contract." His voice dropped, his words obviously intended just for her. "That isn't fair, either, but I meant the timing. I came by this afternoon to see you, Holly. I, ah, I found out I'd been mistaken about something, and I came by to ask you for a date."

"So . . ." She held her breath.

"Do you remember I said once that I'd like to take you to my church sometime?"

"I thought you'd forgotten."

"Look, I really have been busy. And, well, I guess I misunderstood . . ."

Holly knew what he meant. "Rumors have a way of spreading in small towns," she said, smiling.

"Well, anyhow, you seem to like contemporary Christian music, and we have a good group coming Sunday night. If you're free . . ."

"I'm free, Philip," she assured him.

"Then may I pick you up Sunday evening, about 6:30?"

"I'll be ready."

"I won't be going to church with you tonight," Holly explained to her parents on Sunday afternoon. "Philip's asked me to go with him to hear a gospel group."

94

Ron smiled, but Ellen bit her lip in silent disapproval.

"It's just that he said something the night we went to the concert about my having some misconceptions about Pentecostals," Holly went on, trying to ease her mother's concern. "He wants to show me what they're really like."

Holly went upstairs to dress, but her mother followed. "Holly," she said softly as she knocked on the bedroom door, "mind if I come in?"

"Sure." Holly laid a pale green cotton knit on her bed and turned toward her mother. "What's the trouble?"

"No trouble, but . . ."

"But you'd rather I didn't date Philip DeLaCruz. Mom, you're the last person I'd have expected to worry about my dating a Filipino, so what's bothering you?"

"Certainly not that," Ellen responded just a little too quickly. "Did I ever tell you that while I was in nursing school, after your father and I had broken up, I dated a Japanese med student?"

Holly nodded. "Your friend, Kim Ahiro's brother. I know, but nothing came of it. And nothing's likely to come of my dating Philip, either," she added.

"As long as you realize I'm not worried about his race." Ellen zipped up the back of Holly's dress. "But, well, it's easy to get hurt on the rebound."

"And you still hope I'll get back together with Greg, don't you?"

"I'd like to see history repeat itself, Holly, but I know you and I are not the same. And Greg and your father aren't, either. I just want you to be happy."

"Don't worry, Mom." The doorbell rang and Holly recognized Philip's voice. "I promise I'll take it slow and easy," she said. It was as much a warning to herself as a promise to her mother.

Holly had expected to feel uncomfortable at the little Pentecostal church. She didn't mention her fears to Philip, but as he helped her down from his newly purchased pickup she glanced around the rutted parking lot. Curious dark eyes looked at her, as she'd anticipated. But the brown faces wore wide smiles of welcome.

Although many of the members spoke Spanish, the pastor spoke in English, starting with a few announcements, much like those she would have heard in her own church, about Wednesday night Bible study and the Thursday morning Ladies' Mission Society. She shifted uneasily, wondering when someone would do something weird, like speak in tongues or whatever.

She whispered an "amen" when the pastor closed his opening prayer for God's blessing on the service. A few of the amens were more audible, but except for that she might have been sitting beside Greg at First Baptist instead of next to Philip.

The "group" was a quartet that accompanied itself on guitars. They sang mostly in Spanish. Holly congratulated herself on understanding many of the joyful lyrics. *At least I took Spanish for my language requirement though I've forgotten most of what I learned,* she thought. *It's a shame I've used it so little, especially here in Salinas, where half the people speak Spanish as their first language.*

She remembered how many of her friends had studied Spanish, passed the exams, gotten the required credits, and never bothered to speak to their neighbors. *And neither did I. No wonder we don't understand each other.*

She found herself caught up in the rhythmic clapping that accompanied much of the singing. Her hands, too, picked up the infectious beat. Though she couldn't quite bring herself to lift her arms high in praise to God, she almost envied the many, Philip among them, who did.

Mom and Dad and Greg and I love the Lord fully as much as these people, she assured herself. *But somehow we feel uncomfortable with this kind of display.* She watched Philip out of the corner of her eye. His face was turned upward, as were his open palms. The quartet invited the congregation to join in the chorus, and Holly's voice rose with the others.

"I know an interesting place for a light supper," Philip suggested, as he pulled out of the parking lot after the service. "Or have you already had enough cross-cultural experience for one night?"

His tone was light, and she responded in kind. "It's impossible to overdose when cross-cultural food's involved. What kind?"

"Filipino. A place just opened up here in the Alisal." He turned down a side street. She couldn't have been more than a couple of miles from home, yet she didn't recognize the neighborhood. "Do you like lumpia?" he asked.

"Lumpia? I probably do; I like most everything." She laughed. "Just what is lumpia?"

"Well, now, how do I describe it?" It was his turn to chuckle. "Lumpia is sort of a cross between Chinese egg rolls and Mexican tacos. Only better than either one."

She licked her lips. "Two of my favorite dishes," she assured him. "Lead on."

The storefront proclaimed itself "Restaurante Manila." Philip pulled out a cane-seated chair for her at a tiny table and went to the counter. When he returned he carried a large plate filled with plump rolls of translucent pastry. "You thought the United States was a melting pot. Meet the Philippines."

"They look like egg rolls," she said, sniffing the unfamiliar aroma. "But what's inside?"

"Shrimp, chicken, pork." He picked up one of the crisp, steaming delicacies. "Red pepper, onion, garlic."

She took one and bit into it. "Mmmm."

He smiled. "You like them, I gather?" he asked.

She smiled. "Where have they been all my life?" She took another bite. "The pastry is lighter than the Chinese egg rolls I've had," she said, picking up a flaky crumb on the end of her finger and licking it off. "And the filling is so spicy—not hot, really, like Mexican, but, well, tangy."

He seemed delighted with her delight. "Mama always makes them for special occasions, but they've been impossible to buy until this place opened. I'm glad you like them." His voice turned serious. "Did you like our church too? I sensed you felt a little strange, with the clapping and all."

"It was different for me," she admitted. "I think of church as a place to sit quietly and listen. But the Bible does tell us to make a joyful noise unto the Lord, and that's what I heard tonight. People truly making a joyful noise."

"Noise?"

"Only in the best sense." She swallowed the last of one of the lumpia and picked up another. "The quartet was good, but I guess I was paying more attention to the congregation." *And to you,* she realized. "They were so enthusiastic."

"If people aren't enthusiastic in your church," he queried, "why do they go?"

"We go to worship," she defended. "We sing, and we pray, but, well, we don't think it's appropriate to clap."

"And lift up 'holy hands' as it were?"

"You know, I was really surprised." She realized he was studying her face intently as she spoke. *He wants me to like his church, just like he wants me to like his food.* She chose her words carefully, wanting him to approve of her reaction too. "I'm afraid I expected something pretty extreme—shouting, or crying, or . . . Well, you know."

"The Holy Roller thing." He smiled gently at her. "I know you did. WASPs always do."

She was offended by his use of the ugly epithet. "I can't help it if I happen to be white, Anglo-Saxon, and Protestant. But I'm not a 'WASP'—not the way you said it—smug, self-satisfied, narrow-minded."

"No, you're not." His teasing half-smile reassured her. "If I had thought you'd be too comfortable, I never would have invited you to my church. But you see stereotypes come from both sides of the tracks. Most of us don't know your people any better than you know us."

She felt chastened. *But he did care enough about me to want me to learn about his people. And about him.* "I'm not used to worshiping God the same way you do, Philip," she said softly. "But I don't think the form really matters to God."

They each reached for another lumpia, and their hands touched over the platter. For an instant his closed gently around hers, and she was sorry he dropped it so quickly.

"I think I owe you an explanation for my behavior the last couple of weeks," he began.

She shrugged, trying to be casual. "You've been busy, with the strike and all."

"Not so busy I haven't thought about you." His eyes glowed and she felt heat on her cheeks. "I enjoyed the concert with you so much, and I was going to call you as soon as the rally was over, but then I saw you at the barbecue with Greg."

"I wondered if you decided I was the enemy," she said.

"Don't be silly. That would only have made me want to convert you to the cause," he assured her. "No, someone pointed you out as Greg's fiancée. And, well, you were spoken for, and I was angry that you would date me, or anyone, when . . ."

"A lot of people in Salinas thought Greg and I would marry sometime, Philip. I guess even Greg thought so and probably, if you'd asked me a year ago, I would have said so too."

"I'm old fashioned, Holly. I take engagements seriously."

"So do I. That's why I was never engaged to Greg; I was never *sure* I wanted to marry him. And I finally realized it wasn't fair to him for me to let things drag on."

"Did Greg know you'd gone out with me?"

Holly chewed the last of the lumpia slowly. "I guess not," she admitted. "But we had an understanding, while he was here and I was still in school, that we were both free to date others. Philip . . ." She wanted so much to make him understand she hadn't been unfaithful to Greg, but how? "Don't worry," she assured him with a less than totally honest smile. "It wasn't your irresistible charm that broke us up."

Chapter Twelve

*D*espite the disturbing news of picketing in the fields and isolated incidents of violence, Holly floated through the next few days. Mrs. Jones's reticulocyte count skyrocketed, and Holly rejoiced at having a part in her recovery. At the little clinic in Soledad she helped Paul diagnose and treat bladder infections and strep throat and iron-deficiency anemias. The fat, brown babies who came there thrived, and she felt needed.

Philip was out in the fields every day. He didn't march the picket lines himself but drove from farm to farm, watching for trouble and encouraging the striking workers. He made time to stop by the clinic one Wednesday to take Holly out to supper when she'd finished her afternoon's work.

"You said you liked Chinese," he said, as they entered the little restaurant.

They talked over their steaming egg drop soup. "It's so sad, Philip," Holly told him. "My Uncle Ted might have agreed to an election by now if the pact had held up. But he feels caught in the middle. He's stubborn. Lots of the independents are. These incidents aren't doing your union any good."

He nodded grimly. "Chavez is adamantly nonviolent, Holly. But we are being provoked. That's what I'm doing every day: watching for growers, Teamster organizers, anyone who might make trouble, and trying to head them off."

"Can you honestly say all the troublemakers are on the other side?" she asked softly.

"I wish I could, but we have our hotheads too. Sometimes they fight back because someone tries to shove them around. Sometimes it's a misunderstanding. Somebody bends over, and somebody else thinks he's picking up a rock. Somebody scratches an itch, and somebody else thinks he's reaching for a knife or a gun. And, yes, sometimes somebody just picks a fight."

"Be careful, Philip. It would be so easy for someone to be seriously hurt."

"I hope none of our people starts anything, but I can't promise. Drive people up against a wall, and things just might go wrong. My job is to keep things cool."

"You know, I'm not so worried about the farm workers themselves. It's some of the kids I see out on the lines, like my cousin Judy."

"Kid?" he interrupted. "Just how much older are you than Judy?"

"In years?" She smiled. "Only one. But she gets so crazy over things."

"You're not one of those people who thinks 'dedication' is a dirty word, are you?"

"Of course not." She remembered something Vic had said about her. "Somebody told me once that I was afraid to get involved—that I was like a plastic rosebud, afraid I'd melt if I ever got too warm. But that's wrong. I . . ."

"Real rosebuds need warmth," he whispered. "It's what makes them bloom."

She felt her cheeks flush, but he went on immediately. "There's nothing wrong with being dedicated, if the cause is right."

"And you stay in control," she added. "You're dedicated, but you keep things in perspective. Judy gets so carried away, so hysterical."

He nodded. "I know what you mean. Some of the wilder ones scare me a little too."

He served Holly pungent Kung Pau Chicken from the platter the waiter had placed on the table. "I don't know how to ask you this," he said after a few minutes. "It's about Judy and some of her friends. Can I be perfectly frank with you?"

"Of course," she answered, but he still hesitated. She recalled her fears and anticipated his question. "Philip, do you know some of them are using drugs?" she asked.

He nodded. "I hated to bring it up, especially with Judy being your cousin. I haven't any real evidence. I probably wouldn't go to the police anyhow." He sipped his tea. "Wouldn't our opponents love to get hold of a story like that? I can see the headlines: 'Farm workers' union cover for drug dealers.'"

"If it's true . . ." Holly countered.

"Of course it's not true! Cesar Chavez wouldn't tolerate drugs, and I guarantee nobody close to him condones

103

it. But those kids . . . You know what some of them came out of."

"Too well," she told him. "I've tried to talk to Judy."

"For whatever good it does, I'm keeping my eye on them."

"That makes me feel better," Holly told him. "But you can't be everywhere. College classes will start soon, and you'll be teaching full time, won't you?"

"Another week." He frowned. "For a while I hoped the strike would be over by then. It could have been, if the co-op and the Teamsters had just honored the pact." He pushed away a half-full plate. "But as you say, classes start soon. Then my first obligation will be to my students."

"Aren't you afraid you'll be bored with just teaching?"

"Not likely." He almost laughed, and Holly realized she'd never heard him really laugh. "Besides, I'll still be working with the union in my spare time. And it's only for a year."

"Only a year? Why? Don't you think they'll keep you on at the college?" she teased.

"Probably not, once the board gets wind of the fact that I'm working with Chavez." The half-smile came back. "But, no, I'm only temporary anyhow, replacing a teacher who's on sabbatical. A year from now I hope to be on my way to South America."

"South America?" *Kathy said something about his wanting to be a missionary,* she remembered. "To teach there?"

"In a way. I took this job to tide me over while I finish my dissertation and get my doctorate, but what I've always wanted to do is go to South America and teach modern farming techniques. Most of the people who live there haven't a prayer of ever having enough to eat without our help."

"Like with the Peace Corps?"

He nodded. "I once thought I'd join the Peace Corps. But then I found Jesus, and I knew I had to serve him. So I've applied to a few parachurch groups that do relief work in cooperation with evangelical missions. You know, I feed the body while they feed the soul. A couple of agencies are starting long-term programs. I expect I'll hear something definite by spring."

"How exciting." A picture flashed in her mind of Philip spreading fertilizer on the altiplano, and of herself beside him. Holly had never, ever—even as a little girl in Sunday school—pictured herself as anything so heroic as a missionary. She rejected the idea as quickly as it had come. "But why South America? Surely you could do as much good closer to home."

That unsettling glow had come back to his eyes. "Have you ever been sure, absolutely sure, for no good reason whatsoever, that you were destined for something? That's how this is for me."

The waiter brought the check, and Philip reached for it. "My, but this has turned into a sober evening. If you don't have any plans for Saturday night, I'd like another chance. I'll try to make it more lively."

"Saturday night sounds great," she assured him. "But don't try to change too much. I can't imagine a better way to spend an evening than finding out all these surprising things about you."

He called Saturday afternoon. "I'm sorry about to-

night, Holly, but things are getting nasty. Somebody—
the co-op, one of the big corporations, maybe even the
Teamsters—has brought in a bunch of hired thugs.
There's a meeting tonight, and I have to be there. We
have to plan our strategy."

"Of course," she said flatly. "You have to be there."

"Holly, I am sorry. Can I call you again, when things
quiet down a little?"

"Sure." She felt her eyes filling. *Sure, whenever that
might be.* "Philip, it's going to get worse, isn't it?"

"Dear God, I hope not."

She knew the words were the prayer of his heart, as
they were of hers. *At least*, she thought, *school will be
starting next week, and he won't have time to be so involved.*
"Philip, I'll be praying for peace. Take care of yourself."

Holly was startled when Philip slipped into her pew
the next day as the evening service began. "Just returning your visit of last week," he whispered.

The evening hour was sparsely attended. Most of the
scattered worshipers turned to look at the strikingly
handsome young man who sat beside Holly. Her parents
nodded in welcome; so did most of the others. If a few of
the glances seemed quizzical, well, visitors were a rarity
on Sunday evening in Salinas.

Everyone there had known Holly for years. After
Pastor Bishop had asked for "a just resolution to our
present local conflict" in his closing prayer, they clustered around her as she introduced "a friend of mine,
Philip DeLaCruz." They smiled; most of them offered a
hand, and Philip returned their smiles and shook the
proffered hands firmly.

Philip suggested a drive. "It's been so warm today, and I thought it would be nice to go over to Monterey and watch the sunset."

She had almost forgotten the heat wave in the warmth of his nearness. "I'd love that," she answered. "Not too late, though. I have to be at work at seven."

"I'm afraid I have to be out early too." He sighed, and she saw that his dark eyes were tired, though they seemed to brighten when he looked at her. "It's been bad, and it's going to get worse," he admitted. "But this evening is mine, to refresh myself, renew myself for what's coming."

And he wants to spend it with me. Her heart began to sing, and it didn't stop even when she heard the whispers as they left the church. "DeLaCruz? Must be Mexican." "Filipino, maybe?" "Haven't I seen him on the TV news, with that man Chavez?"

And she heard her mother's determined response. "Holly works with his mother. And he seems to be a very nice young man."

The sun dipped into the sapphire bay. Ribbons of purple, ruby, and rose spread out at the fading juncture of sea and sky, and a large pearl moon rose behind a wind-beaten cypress. Philip had said very little during the half-hour drive, and Holly was content just to be close to him as they walked hand in hand along the narrow strip of damp sand at the edge of the breaking waves.

They came to a cluster of low boulders just above the tide pools and, still without words, sat to watch the last bit of the sun disappear. Holly's foot felt something alien, and almost without thinking she kicked sand over an empty beer can. "God is so good," she breathed, turning again to the sunset.

"In spite of our efforts to mess things up," he muttered, completing with his own foot the simple burial.

"Do you want to talk about it?" Holly asked, when the last glow had faded to the west. "You don't have to, but if it would help . . ."

"I don't want to spoil the evening," he whispered. "Especially for you. I want your life to be beautiful."

"Nothing could spoil it, Philip. The sunset, the surf, the breeze, the moon. It's never been lovelier."

"All this beauty puts things in perspective. I need to be reminded, sometimes, how small our problems really are next to God's greatness." His hand found hers in the darkness. "I'm having trouble remembering that right now."

"It will work itself out, Philip. Soon everybody will realize that we all want the same things. The growers and the workers can both win, if they only talk to each other."

"There's been too much talk already," he said softly. The gentle surf sloshed against the sand. "What we need is more listening." He uncovered the empty beer can, picked it up, and dropped it in a trash container as they walked back to the car.

Chapter Thirteen

As Philip had predicted, things got even uglier in the fields. The court called the strike a "jurisdictional dispute" and ruled it illegal. More of the major corporate farms signed with the powerful Teamsters' Union. The field workers felt they had been betrayed, and no piece of paper issued by a judge could force them to harvest the rotting crops.

Every day the newspaper reported one or two incidents. A deputy sheriff arrested a handful of UFW pickets who blocked Ted Hanlon's driveway. Sam McLean, angry when the laborers left his ripe crops, brandished a heavy wrench he carried to open the irrigation pipes, vowing he would defend his right to run his own business to the death if necessary.

The rusty, battered cars of the UFW were often found, early in the morning, with their tires slashed. But so were the shiny pickups of the growers. Tempers grew hotter. The old sedans had mysterious accidents that their drivers said were not accidents. But the highway patrol never seemed to find the shiny cars with new dents that, the UFW insisted, were forcing UFW organizers off dusty lanes into muddy irrigation ditches.

The towns were ominously quiet. The rumbling, grumbling, heavily loaded flatbed trucks that normally filled the summer streets of Greenfield and Soledad and Gonzales sat idle beside the fields. The alleys that wound between the packing sheds beside the railroad tracks in Salinas were nearly empty.

At the hospital, the administration ordered disaster drills. Employees "bloodied" with catsup were bandaged by their coworkers. Tom Tanner, the chief tech, circulated his out-of-date emergency call-back roster, and Holly, along with the others, filled in her home phone number and confirmed that of the person below her on the chain.

Kathy laughed. "You'd think we were expecting an invasion. Why Greg told me just the other night that Chavez's people wouldn't dare do anything in daylight now, what with the guards the farmers' association has brought in."

So she and Greg are still seeing each other, Holly mused. "We've been lucky so far that nobody's been seriously hurt," she said, recalling Philip's warning about pushing people too far. "Let's pray it stays that way."

"I still think this 'emergency' stuff is just the bureaucracy's way of justifying its own existence," Kathy muttered.

"It never hurts to be ready," Tom assured them. Med techs tended to be an independent lot, and Tom Tanner's hardest job was acting as a buffer between his disdainful staff and the "higher-ups." "Besides," he told them, "one of these days, some nosy TV reporter is going to crash a helicopter into some place he had no business being, and we'll have to save his life."

Though the hospital's emergency preparations proved unnecessary, Holly's Uncle Paul patched up a few ugly scrapes and stitched up a cut forehead or two nearly every day.

Holly went down to the Soledad clinic on Tuesday, as she did several afternoons a week. As he often did, Philip dropped by and stuck his head into her stuffy kitchen-lab.

"How are you holding up?" he asked, reaching up to tilt the fan that sat on top of the refrigerator so that its breeze blew toward the stool in front of her microscope. "It will cool off soon," he promised.

"That's what I keep telling myself." Holly slipped the small glass counting chamber off the microscope stage and cleaned it. She picked up another tube of blood, sucked a tiny sample up to a line on a tiny pipette, filled the pipette with diluting fluid, and began shaking it between her thumb and forefinger.

"I never saw anybody do that over at the hospital lab," he commented.

She chuckled. "Only when the Coulter Counter breaks down and we're desperate. This is the old-fashioned way to do blood counts." She deftly put the pipette tip to the edge of the counting chamber, letting the diluted blood sample flow smoothly into place. "I used to wonder why they made us learn how, but I'm sure glad now."

"It looks like it would take a lot of practice to do it right."

"It does. I never got very good when I was training. Nobody ever thought we'd need it. But I've had lots of practice the last few weeks."

"That's good." He glanced around the makeshift laboratory. "You never know when it might come in handy."

"To be honest, if I never have to do another manual blood count, it will be too soon." She slipped the counting chamber onto the microscope stage, picked up a palm-sized mechanical counter, and began clicking furiously. "The Coulter Counter is faster, easier, and more accurate."

"But not always available," he reminded her. "By the way, not to change the subject, but if you're going to be finished soon, I have a supper invitation for you. My mother suggested I bring you home with me."

"Oh, Philip, it sounds great, but on a work night? Surely she doesn't want to cook for company after working all day."

"She wouldn't have asked if she didn't want you to come," he assured her. "One more person isn't that much trouble, anyhow. Papa or one of the kids almost always brings somebody home." His eyes danced as he smiled assurance. "It's that kind of home."

Holly chuckled. "My mom's always ready for company, too, but she does like to be forewarned."

"Honest, it was Mama's idea. She likes you."

"I like her, too, Philip. Okay. I'll be finished here in five minutes."

The DeLaCruz homestead was as unlike the Hanlon place as two farms less than five miles apart could be. Strawberry plants poked through planting holes and sprawled dark green over the black plastic mulch that covered the soil. The shiny film protected the precious fruit from the damp soil and focused the sun's rays to encourage ripening.

A low, tile-roofed pink stucco house squatted in the middle of the berry fields, shaded by a small orchard. Holly recognized Cici's car parked behind a dusty pickup on a wide spot in the graveled driveway.

Cici met them on the front step. "Oh, good. You came, Holly," she said, arms open in welcome. "Come on in. Supper's almost ready."

The rooms were surprisingly cool. A wide overhang protected the windows from the afternoon sun, and the thick cement-block walls held out the heat much as the adobe of a century before had. "I've got a fan going in the living room." Cici waved her hand as she breezed back into the kitchen. "Your papa's in there," she said to Philip.

The wiry little man Holly had seen with them the day of the rally lifted himself from the low couch and offered a callused hand as Philip introduced Holly to Julio. His smile, wide and warm as his wife's, cut through the leathery folds of his weather-beaten face. "I've heard so many nice things about you," he told her.

Holly heard Cici call down the hallway, and a younger edition of Philip appeared from one of the bedrooms. "My brother, John," Philip said. As Julio ushered them into the dining room a slim teenager Holly identified as Angela, the youngest DeLaCruz, set plates of crisp salad at each place.

"How do you do it?" Holly asked Cici later, as Angela came back from the kitchen with plates of a caramel-drenched custard that Philip called "lichee flan." "I know how hard you work all day, and then to come home and cook a meal like this?"

Cici's openhanded gesture implied it was no effort at all. "I've done it all my life, and Angela helps a lot. Besides, you work nearly every afternoon at the clinic."

"Mama wouldn't know what to do with herself if she couldn't cook," Philip explained. "It's her hobby."

Julio smiled proudly. "It's why I chose her," he said. "She was the best cook in her village."

"You always told me it was because I was the prettiest," Cici teased.

"That too," her husband assured her.

"The fact is he was desperate," Cici told Holly in a stage whisper. "All those years in America, with no good Filipina for a wife. Those Filipino-American soldiers went through our village like locusts."

"It was right at the end of World War II," Philip explained. "Many Filipino men came here to work in the fields in the late 1920s, after the Japanese exclusion acts, my father among them. But they neglected to bring any women with them."

"Back then," Julio interrupted, "it was unthinkable for us to mix with the whites. We planned, most of us, to go home again, money in our pockets, and find our brides there. But the money seemed to run through our fingers. And then the war came."

"My Julio, and many of the others, joined the army

and came to liberate us from the Japanese. At least . . ." She winked at Holly. "At least they said they came to liberate the Philippines. But I think they were looking for brides. On the day I married Julio, there were ten weddings in our little village church. In one day!"

Holly studied the happy faces around the table. "I hope they all turned out as well as yours."

"I do too." Julio's eyes scanned the room as well. "The United States granted citizenship to all of us and full veterans' benefits. We've had a good life here. Better," he added sadly, "than many who have come since to work in these fields."

"No politics!" Cici demanded. "Holly is here so we can get acquainted. And have a good time." She stacked the dishes, and Angela started to pick them up. "Leave the dishes for later," her mother told her. "Papa, get your guitar, and Angela will sing for our guest."

"Please don't think you have to entertain me," Holly protested.

Cici waved her objections aside. "Nonsense. I like to show her off."

Holly marveled at the family's easy hospitality. *We'd never do this at home*, she reflected as each, in turn and together, played, sang, danced. *They're so totally unself-conscious*. She was startled to find herself joining in a lively refrain.

"I don't know where the time went," she said to Philip as he drove her back to the clinic to pick up her car. "Is your family always like that?"

"Like what?"

"So, well, relaxed, comfortable."

"Why not?" he asked. "We're family."

"I'm not," she reminded him. "But you made me feel like I was."

"I'm glad," he said softly. "I hope you'll come again."

He didn't stop by on Thursday, and she told herself it was best. *He's good for me. He makes me think,* she told herself, knowing full well that it wasn't intellectual stimulation that made her shiver at the thought of his tender smile, his fiery eyes, his low but commanding voice. *But things are moving too fast. I mustn't let myself get too close to him.*

She was doing blood counts again on Friday when she heard his step behind her. "Hi. Can I bother you for just a minute?" he asked casually.

She continued clicking her hand counter for a moment, then stopped. "Sure." She turned, returning his smile. "How are things going?"

"As usual. A few petty confrontations, but most of the action is in the courts right now. I just stopped by to ask if you had any plans for Sunday afternoon. I thought we might go over to Monterey again if the warm weather holds."

"I'd like that, but I finally talked Judy into coming to Sunday dinner at my folks'." She saw the disappointment on his face. "It's important, Philip. She needs me, whether she knows it or not."

His smile faded but only for an instant. "Of course it's important. This is the first time she's agreed to see any of her family except you, isn't it?"

She nodded. "Pray for me, Philip. And for her—especially for her—pray that we can reach her. She seems so terribly lost for all her brave talk about finding herself."

Chapter Fourteen

Holly's parents were obviously trying not to pressure Judy. Ron asked if she planned to go back and finish college.

"Maybe," Judy grudgingly answered.

"Holly said you were in New York last winter, and Detroit. How did you like the snow?" Ellen asked.

"It's no worse than the rain."

"Are you planning on staying in the valley for a while?" from Ron.

"As long as Cesar needs me."

"Don't you like the roast beef?" Ellen asked. "You've scarcely touched it. Can I get you something else?"

"No, thanks. I don't eat much meat anymore."

They kept trying, but Judy toyed with the wholesome home-cooked meal and spoke only in direct answer to their questions.

Holly helped her mother clear the table, and Judy followed them into the kitchen. She stood by, awkwardly, as Holly began washing the dishes. "Dish towel's on the back of the door, where it's always been," Holly reminded her. "Remember the rule. Mom cooks; I wash the dishes; you dry them."

"It's okay," Ellen said, reaching for the towel herself. "Judy's company now."

"No." Judy took the towel from Ellen's hand. "But it's been a long time," she apologized. "I think I've forgotten where things go."

"You used to be as much at home in this kitchen as in your mother's," Ellen reminded her. Judy flinched, still, at the mention of her dead mother, and Ellen gave her a warm hug. "We've missed you."

"Have you?" Judy pulled from Ellen's embrace. "I didn't think anybody around here missed me."

Holly looked up, startled. "You know we're all glad to have you back."

Judy's shrill whine suddenly increased in volume. "Didn't you tell them I came back to drag you all out of your comfy little ruts and make you share your precious profits with the people who do the work?"

"Judy!" The words themselves hadn't shocked her, but Holly had never expected her cousin to say them to her mother.

Ellen opened her mouth, then closed it again.

"It's true, you know," Judy insisted. "When was the last time you went out into those fields and saw where all that money comes from?"

"Holly told us you were working with Chavez, Judy. Has she also told you that McLean-Hanlon is almost evenly divided on the question of signing with the UFW—in spite of the fact that we barely broke even last year and will almost certainly lose money this year?"

They finished the dishes in silence. "Maybe you'd better take me home," Judy said to Holly.

"Please, Judy," Ellen protested. "You know we'd like you to stay longer. There's lots of family gossip to catch up on."

Judy shook her head. "I have to get back. I don't belong to the family anymore anyhow."

"Holly doesn't believe that; neither do I; neither, by the way, does your Great-Aunt Carrie."

"I should have known Marianne would tell her I was in town." Judy's pale face grew paler. "Oh, you know I always loved Aunt Carrie. I suppose I should go see her. But they haven't told my father, have they?"

"I'm sure they haven't," Holly interrupted. "Marianne knows how you feel, and she wouldn't violate your confidence."

"Marianne hasn't told him, and neither has Mother," Ellen assured her, "though we all know he'd welcome you with open arms if you would only go to him."

"That will be the day." Judy's laugh, like her voice, was nervously high-pitched. "Holly, I really need to get back to Soledad."

"You had no right to talk to her that way," Holly protested as she pulled onto the freeway. "Mom really is on your side, just as Aunt Marianne and Grandma Carrie are—and Uncle Harry, too, for that matter."

"Then why hasn't McLean-Hanlon signed? Oh, I know; my dear daddy's being stubborn, and your Uncle Ted's sitting on his duff waiting for the problem to go away."

"I can't say I approve of your sarcasm. Still," Holly

had to admit grudgingly, "you do seem to have summed up the situation pretty well."

"Holly, sometimes I think you and your mother and the people like you are worse than my father. You mean well, but you think if you just throw a bone to the poor now and then and say your prayers on Sunday the good Lord will reward you by preserving your precious status quo."

Holly resisted the impulse to cover her ears as Judy's wail echoed in the little car.

"Can't you see the status quo is wrong?" Judy ranted on. "No, of course you can't, or you'd be out there with us on the picket lines."

"I may not be on the picket lines, but I am working almost every afternoon at the clinic," Holly reminded her.

Judy's voice softened. "Are you really working at the clinic because you think the union's right or just so you can see Philip DeLaCruz?"

"Don't be silly," Holly protested. "I've only known Philip for a few weeks."

"He's awfully good looking. And awfully nice too."

"Yes, he is," Holly agreed.

"We miss him in the fields now that he's teaching," Judy went on. "He's always so quiet, but people listen to him. You know, I almost got arrested a couple of weeks ago, but he talked the cops into letting us off with a warning."

"Arrested! Again?"

"Don't get all self-righteous on me. We weren't doing anything. It was just that silly stuff about the strike being illegal."

"How can you help anybody if you're in jail?"

"They never lock anybody up for long. They don't have room." Judy shrugged as Holly stopped in front of the shabby house. "Besides, the beds in jail are better than sleeping bags."

"You would know, wouldn't you? Wasn't being in jail in San Francisco bad enough?"

Judy shrugged. "We were only locked up for one night, in a holding tank. We didn't have any beds at all. But Vic says it isn't so bad."

"Vic? You said he was still in Detroit."

"Yeah. He'll be out in a couple more weeks, though."

"Out? Judy, Vic isn't in jail, is he?"

"It wasn't anything, really," Judy insisted. "He got caught with a few pills."

"Amphetamines?" Holly thought again of Judy's lack of appetite, her moodiness, her overreacting. "You're still using drugs, aren't you? You know what that stuff can do to you. You promised me you'd stay away from it."

"Oh, don't be an old fuddy-duddy, cousin. A little speed never hurt anybody." Judy opened the car door. "You and Phil make a good pair. He doesn't approve of us either, you know. I guess Cesar'd tell us to get lost, too, but nobody tells him what goes on after hours. He needs all the help he can get, even if we do pop some pills now and then."

Holly had guessed, but Judy's brazen admission still jarred her. "A few pills! You aren't stupid. You know 'speed kills' isn't just a catchy phrase."

"You don't believe all that propaganda, do you? All my friends do drugs, and we're all just fine."

"Are you?" Holly watched her cousin move toward

the car's open door. "Judy, I love you. And God loves you. Please let us help you get your life back on track."

"God doesn't love people who live like I do, Holly. You said so yourself once. Besides, I happen to like the track I'm on." Judy got out of the car and leaned through the open window. Her parting words were icy cold on the warm wind. "It's my life, and you and Phil and my father and everybody else who wants to tell me what to do can go to the devil."

Holly watched, wordless, as her cousin walked up the cracked sidewalk onto the sagging porch. *Oh, God,* she prayed, *show me how to get her out of this.*

"Aunt Marianne, I have to talk to you this afternoon, alone," Holly whispered as they passed in the narrow hallway of the clinic late the next afternoon.

A few minutes later Marianne stepped into the kitchen and closed the door behind her. "What is it, Holly? You sounded so serious. If it's a problem with a patient, Paul will be available in a few minutes."

"I wish it were." Holly recapped the bottle of urine test strips in her hand. "It's about Judy."

"I've been worried about her too." Marianne sat down on the stool Holly offered. "I'm so glad she's at least talking to you."

"I don't know if she will anymore, though. I suspected she was using drugs, and I confronted her about it last night."

The older woman nodded sadly. "I'm afraid quite a few of those kids are. We counsel them, if they come to us. But we can't help them if they don't want to be helped."

"I think she does want help, though. Oh, she says she's just great, but deep down, underneath, she's desperate. I just feel like I have to get her away from those kids she's staying with."

"It won't be easy." Marianne folded her hands as if in prayer, a habit Holly had noticed before. "Maybe I shouldn't tell you this, but I know you're Judy's friend, maybe the only real friend she has, and I think you can do more for her if you know the whole story."

"There's more? More than dropping out of college? More than tramping all over the country, living in one commune after another? Using drugs? Living with a man who's been arrested for possession?"

Marianne quietly added, "Did you know she has a daughter?"

Holly gasped. "A baby!" *She must have been pregnant when she left Berkeley*, Holly realized. *And she didn't confide in me*, she thought sadly. "How old?" she asked.

"About three months."

"And she never said a word to me, in Berkeley, or since she's been here."

"She was probably afraid to tell you, for fear she'd lose your friendship."

Holly nodded sadly. "But she's out picketing all the time. Who takes care of the baby?"

"They take turns. There are several children living in that place. It's hard to believe, given the conditions there, but the kids are in pretty good shape."

"Thank God for that, at least. But, especially if there are children there, don't we have to do something?"

"About the drugs? What can we do? Holly, we're bound by medical ethics."

Holly remembered Philip's words. "And if word got out it could kill the union."

Marianne nodded. "There are people in the leadership, or near it at least, who know. But they're afraid to go to the authorities because of the scandal."

"You say we're bound by ethics, but Judy's not my patient. My knowledge isn't medical information; it's personal."

"True," Marianne admitted. "If you want to be technical about it."

"And isn't there a greater wrong, sometimes, than violating confidentiality?"

"I've asked that question myself, but no. We have to honor their privacy. If our patients can't trust us, they won't come to us at all."

"Maybe." Holly thought about Judy, and her baby, and the other children. "But we can't let a bunch of druggies risk the lives of helpless children and just do nothing."

She thought she heard a noise in the hall. A door latch opening or closing. Marianne put a finger to her lips. Holly went to the door, but the hallway was empty.

"Sometimes," Marianne said very quietly, "there is nothing we can do but pray and wait and be available."

Classes had started at the college, and Philip had rented a small apartment in Salinas. Holly was glad that he no longer patrolled the dusty farm roads looking for trouble, though she wondered if, perhaps, his absence had something to do with the escalation of violence in the fields.

"I doubt it," he told her when she made the suggestion over lumpia one Sunday evening late in September.

"There's so much tension. We have evidence that either the Teamsters or some of the growers, or both, have brought in paid troublemakers."

She nodded. "My Uncle Ted calls them 'guards' of course."

"I guess it depends, at least in part, on your point of view. But they're a bad bunch, Holly, and violence only begets more violence."

"Maybe it's selfish of me, but I'm glad you're not out there every day anymore," she said. "Who'd treat me to lumpia if you got hurt?" she added with a grin, nibbling at the spicy pastry. "So, are you bored to death yet with teaching?"

"It's certainly different," he conceded. "But, no, not boring, not yet at least. I like the kids. And I like the questions they ask—things they wouldn't ask of someone older. I'm from their generation, from an ethnic minority, and a known supporter of liberal causes. When I tell them to take it easy, when I talk nonviolence, they listen."

"And you can set an example. All they hear is that 'everybody does it' whatever wild, crazy, thing 'it' may be." She paused. "Like Judy."

"Have you seen her lately?" he asked.

"Not since that Sunday," she said sadly. "Philip, she admitted she's using speed. She said they all do drugs."

"Not all of them, thank God. But that house she's living in—several of us are concerned about it. If it weren't for the possible scandal, we'd throw them out. Maybe we should anyhow—tell Cesar, and have him openly disavow them before the police find out, not to mention the local press. Especially now that Vic Bigelow's turned up."

"Vic! Vic's here?"

"You don't know him, do you? He's a born loser."

"Judy said he was coming, but I kept hoping he'd just disappear, get out of her life and give her a chance. He's been in jail for possession."

"I know. He was working in New York on the grape boycott when he first got into trouble. We fired him, but I heard he was arrested for dealing later, in Detroit. Fortunately for us, nobody there connected him to the UFW. But I'm sure the *Salinas Californian* would love to give him front-page treatment. What has he got to do with your cousin, though?"

She poked at the crumbs on her plate, hating to tell him the rest of the bad news about Judy. *As if he hasn't heard it all before,* she told herself. She swallowed her pride. "Vic Bigelow is the reason Judy's where she is. She met him in Berkeley. She idolized him. He used her, gave her drugs, dragged her into his student demonstrations. They were—still are, I guess—lovers."

"I see. I knew one of the babies was Judy's, but I just never connected her to Vic. I'm sorry."

"They met in Berkeley. I introduced them. Can you believe it?"

"Do you know him well?"

"No. I just went to a couple of meetings about the grape boycott. Then I realized that he was just using his causes to get power for himself."

"And customers, maybe," Philip mused aloud.

"Oh, Philip, I should have tried harder to persuade her to drop him—especially when I realized he was giving her drugs. We grew up together. She knew right from wrong. What happened?"

"What happened to any of them? And why didn't it happen to us?"

"I wonder that myself, sometimes. I guess, but for the grace of God . . . That's it for me anyhow. I believe in him, so I believe in absolute right and wrong. Judy did once too."

"We spend a lot of time trying to reform the world, don't we?" he said. "Trying to save blacks and whites from each other; children from poverty; young people from drugs and immorality; labor from management. I have this crazy notion that I'm here to save the peasants of the altiplano from hunger. But maybe the answer is more basic than that."

Holly was puzzled. "Isn't that the Christian ideal? That we are here to help others?"

"I never paid a lot of attention to my catechism, but I seem to recall something about our ultimate purpose being to love and to serve God. Jesus said the first commandment was to love God."

"But we serve him by serving one another."

"Yes, of course." He seemed to be struggling with a paradox he couldn't quite unravel. "But people need to change, and we can't change them. Only God can do that."

"I guess you're right," she confessed. "But please pray with me that he'll change Judy."

He took her hand in his then, and they bowed their heads and prayed together.

Chapter Fifteen

The drug raid was on the evening news two days later. Her parents watched openmouthed, and a sick knot formed in Holly's stomach as the pictures flickered on the TV screen. The thin young woman with scraggly red hair tried to shield her face with her hands as the on-scene reporter shoved his camera at her, but the Stevenses all recognized Judy.

". . . Sheriff's department, in response to an anonymous tip, raided a derelict house on Soledad's east side," the in-studio announcer said over the images. "Substantial amounts of illegal drugs and drug paraphernalia were confiscated. Nearly twenty men and women, and several children, were living in the small, dirty house. They are reputed to be associated with the UFW organizers," he concluded, "though union sources deny knowledge of any drug-related activity." Holly didn't imagine the smugness in his voice.

"I've got to go to her. Maybe we can get her out on

bail or something." Holly started for the door, but her father held her back.

"They undoubtedly have lawyers by now, and I doubt we could do anything until morning. I promise I'll call then and post bail if necessary," Ron said.

"Bring her home with you," Ellen offered. "She can stay with us as long as she needs to while she gets help. Holly, you didn't know anything about this, did you?"

"I'm afraid I did," Holly admitted. "I guessed, at first, because of the way she was acting, but she admitted it the other night when I took her home. I hoped, we all hoped, we could stop it before something like this happened."

"We? I gather this was an open secret," Ron commented.

"Marianne knew, but of course being a nurse she couldn't say anything." Holly explained. "Philip was suspicious. He didn't know anything for sure, and besides, he was afraid the media would use it against the union."

"He's right," Ron said. "This will hurt the UFW badly, and not just with their opposition. Most of the field workers hate drugs as much as we do."

"It's Judy we have to worry about right now, not the union," Ellen reminded them. "Maybe you should try to call her, Holly. At least she'd know we care about her."

Holly started for the phone in the hall, but it rang before she could pick it up. "That was fast," Marianne's familiar voice commented.

"I was about to call the jail, Marianne, to see if I could talk to Judy."

"You'd better not," Marianne said firmly. "I spoke with her earlier, and . . ."

"Oh, good. What can we do to help?"

"She called me about the baby. They took all the children to Juvenile Hall, and she hoped I could get her out."

"You can, can't you?"

"Not tonight. But I can probably persuade the authorities to let us have temporary custody tomorrow morning. Hopefully we can get Judy released, too, if we can raise bail."

"Dad's already offered. And Judy could come here." She dropped her voice to a whisper. "Mom and Dad don't know about the baby yet, but . . ."

"I just told my mother the whole story, and, as she says, we have plenty of room. Besides, the uniform might help." She chuckled. "The courts still look kindly on the Salvation Army, and Paul and I have had plenty of experience in using their favor—also, I might add, in looking after wayward girls and their children."

"You're probably right. But I'll do anything I can. Be sure and tell Judy I still want to help."

"Holly, you're the last person Judy wants to see right now. And, well, I hate to ask this, because I can't believe you would, but it wasn't you who called the sheriff, was it?"

"Me!"

"I didn't think you would, not after our talk, and certainly not anonymously. But Judy thinks you did. Someone, one of the other kids who got arrested, told her you were the one who turned them in. Holly, I'll try to convince her it wasn't you, but for now you'd better stay away."

Holly blinked back hot tears. "How could she ever

think I'd betray her?" she sniffed. "We used to be so close."

"I'm sure she thinks you meant to help, but right now she's terribly bitter. She may lose custody of little Carrie." Marianne paused. "I guess you didn't know. She named her baby after Mom—another Caroline McLean. And there's more bad news. The baby's father . . . He was on parole. He will almost certainly be sent back to Michigan to prison."

"Vic." Holly said flatly, letting her tears fall. "Oh, God, help that poor girl. Help me, help us, to bring her back to you, for her sake, and for little Caroline's."

"Amen," Marianne murmured. "Holly, I'll let you know what happens in the morning."

Holly had gone upstairs to bed, but she could hear Sam McLean's voice clearly. "They've got a lot of nerve!" he shouted. Holly slipped into her robe and went down to the living room where Sam stood bawling out his rage to his cousin and her husband. She took her place beside her mother on the couch, as if to defend Ellen.

"I told you that outfit was no good!" he harangued. "Do you still think McLean-Hanlon should sign a contract with that bunch of Commies and dope fiends?"

"Sam, I know you're upset about Judy. We all are," Ellen soothed. "But it really has nothing to do with the strike."

"What the heck do you think they were doing here? Stirring up trouble in the fields all day, threatening honest people who just want to put in a day's work and collect a day's pay, and then carrying on all over town all night, smoking pot, using that LSD stuff, sleeping around every night."

His ruddy Scots face was crimson with rage, but he had to pause for breath. Ellen pleaded with him to sit down and take it easy.

"Take it easy! You don't know the whole story, do you? My little girl, all I have left." He sat, slumping into the plump easy chair with a groan. "She looks so much like her mother. You know, I'm almost glad Di didn't live to see this day."

"Sam," Ellen protested, "Judy needs you now."

"She sure does. You don't even know how much she does, but it's too late. These so-called friends of hers . . ." He groaned. "She's even got a kid. Did you know that? By that no-good dope dealer she ran off with a year ago. He's on his way back east somewhere for breaking parole, and she's in jail here, and now Marianne tells me one of those poor little babies they've got over at Juvenile Hall is my granddaughter."

"Marianne told you?" Holly questioned, "When?"

"An hour or so ago. She thinks if I go to court with her and Paul tomorrow it will help them get temporary custody of my granddaughter."

"You will help, won't you?" Holly urged. "For the baby's sake at least."

He nodded glumly. "For the baby's sake. Not for Judy's."

"For Judy's too," Ellen urged. "She's your daughter, and she's in trouble."

"When she can come to me and admit how wrong she's been and prove that she wants to change, then, maybe . . ."

He stood up and moved toward the door. "It's late, and I'm keeping you all up. But you've got a right to know, because of the business, where I stand. That union has taken my last child from me, and it will not get my farm."

Sam's blind rage, more than his words, frightened Holly. After he left, she called Philip's apartment, but he didn't answer. She tried the DeLaCruz farm. "I know it's awfully late," she apologized when Cici answered. "But is Philip there? I really need to talk to him."

"You've heard the news, I gather. I'm sorry about your cousin."

"It's been a shock, but it may be the best thing for her in the long run. Maybe it will get her on a different track. But, Cici, that isn't why I called. I need to talk to Philip, and there's no answer at his apartment."

"He's at a union meeting," Cici told her. "Holly," she continued, "I am truly sorry about your cousin, and I know Philip is too. But right now the union is his big worry. This scandal—the union didn't have anything to do with that. Cesar would have thrown them out if he'd known. Now it's all over the TV news, and they're having a big meeting, trying to figure out how to handle the story so it does the least harm to the cause. 'Damage control,' they call it."

"I wish them well. Really," Holly insisted. "In a way that's why I called. Judy's father has been here. He's blaming the union, unreasonable as that is, and he's making threats. I thought Philip should know."

Holly heard Cici's long sigh. "I'm not surprised. Philip and Cesar expected that kind of trouble as well as the bad press. I don't know when I'll hear from him, but when I do, I'll tell him what you said."

"And tell him to be careful. I'll be praying for him."

"And we will be praying for Judy. Good night, Holly."

"Thank you. Good night."

Holly prayed through most of the short night. She pleaded that the Lord would use the latest disaster in her short life to bring Judy back to him. "She was your child," Holly sobbed. "We both accepted Jesus as our Savior the same summer, at camp. Please, Lord, right there in that terrible jail, bring her back to you and to us. And show me how to help her."

She prayed, too, for little Carrie, but she soon felt the calm assurance of the Lord that Judy's baby was in his care.

She felt less comfortable praying about the broader effects of the drug raid. "Lord, I can't believe that you are on the side of either the UFW or the farmers. I know that real justice is found only through you and not in contracts written by us."

She thought of Philip, who was certain he was serving God by aiding Chavez's organizers. "Lord, if the UFW is your agent for justice, then don't let this be used against them. Please, please, help Philip with his damage control." She remembered Sam McLean's rage. "And protect them all. Don't let anyone do anything foolish."

Despite her prayers, fear possessed her. Sam had never mentioned Philip's name, she told herself. Sam didn't even know him. *But he and his family are inexorably involved.* "Lord, don't let Philip be hurt."

She had intended to ask Tom for a few hours off the next morning so she could go to the courthouse and see what she could do for Judy. But there was a flu epidemic. Two other techs called in sick, leaving the lab badly understaffed. She remembered Marianne's comment that Judy somehow blamed her for the raid. *Maybe it's for the best that I can't go to her,* she told herself. *Marianne and Paul can probably handle this better by themselves.*

She called Soledad at lunchtime, but Grandma Carrie had no news yet. "Grandma hasn't heard anything new," Holly reported to a concerned Cici. "Marianne thought, last night, that they could probably get temporary custody of Judy's baby at least. And she hoped Judy would be released on bail and go home with them too."

"That would be good. The judge would probably trust your aunt and uncle, being that they are Salvation Army."

Holly wanted to ask about Philip, but she told herself he would be safely back at the college teaching his classes. The nagging undercurrent of fear, she told herself, was nonsense. "The story in this morning's paper was awful," she said to Cici.

"No worse than we expected, though. The sheriff, at least, seems to have enough common sense to know he can't blame the UFW for the behavior of a few of its volunteers."

It was late afternoon when Marianne called, and Holly was already home from work. She grabbed the phone. "There was no problem about the baby," Marianne told her. "She's sleeping in our old cradle right here beside me. She's healthy, and she's so used to being cared for by different people that she seems perfectly content with us."

"And Judy?" Holly asked.

"That's not so good."

"She's not still in jail is she?"

"No," Marianne replied. "Most of them were released first thing this morning."

"The union didn't post bail for them, did they?"

"No, the union has disavowed them totally," Marianne assured her.

"And rightly so, surely. If they hadn't . . ."

"Yes, it was the only thing they could do. And given what they were doing, the UFW doesn't owe them a thing. No, some public defender got the ones with no prior drug record released on their own recognizance. But she isn't here, not right now anyhow."

"Why not?"

"We begged her to stay with us. She even came home with us and little Carrie. But as soon as she got the baby settled, she took off. She loves that little girl, but she's not herself."

"Speed?" Holly asked. "If she's addicted . . ."

"She was terribly nervous, nearly hysterical. Amphetamines are physically addictive, and she may simply have gone out to find a supply."

"Couldn't the judge have ordered her to stay with you?"

"I don't think so. She's an adult in the eyes of the law. He could, and did, insist the baby remain in our care, but Judy is under no legal restriction other than to stay in the county and to report for trial two weeks from now."

"But why on earth wouldn't she stay with you if the baby's there?"

"I'm really not sure. I told you she blamed you for the raid. From something she said, I think she may blame me too."

"But how could she?"

"Do you remember when we were talking at the clinic and thought we heard someone in the hall? If someone heard just a few words, and then, after the raid, put two and two together and got five, they might have thought one of us called the sheriff—and told Judy so."

"Oh, no. Marianne, I don't think she trusted anyone in this town but you and me and maybe Philip. And now she doesn't trust you or me."

"Or Philip," Marianne added. "She blames the union for not standing behind them on this drug charge."

"That's absurd. How could the UFW support drug abuse?"

"When you're using drugs, you don't always think clearly."

"So she'll leave us, leave her own baby, and go back into that shadow world." Holly shivered. "We have to stop her."

"It may not be as bad as it looks," Marianne offered. "If she just went to find some pills, she may come back here simply because she has no place else to go. And I don't believe she'll go far without the baby."

"What about Vic? Someone said he was wanted in Michigan."

"That's another reason why I'm worried about Judy. He was on parole. This is a parole violation of course, so he's been sent back there. It's true they were never married, but she really seems to care for him. So she blames whoever gave the sheriff that anonymous tip for putting him back in prison, along with everything else."

Marianne paused, and Holly could visualize the familiar folding of hands and bowing of head before she continued. "We must pray for her and trust that God will look after her."

"You're right, of course. But it's so much easier to say we will leave something in God's hands than to do it. I'm afraid I'm not very good at waiting."

She heard Marianne's rueful chuckle and then the sound of a door opening in the background. "Just a minute," the older woman told her. Then an abrupt, "I'll have to call you back later. Judy just came in."

"Thank God," Holly said as she hung up the phone. She relayed the news to her mother. "I guess God knows I don't have much patience," she concluded.

Chapter Sixteen

*P*hilip called after supper, and she shared with him the news about Judy. "Maybe you're right about her," he agreed. "This may be just what she needs to break out of that mess and pick up her life again. I sure hope some good comes out of it, somehow."

"I've heard a little on TV and read tonight's paper. Obviously the authorities realize the union isn't involved."

"Officially this is an entirely separate issue. It's no different than if, say, some employees in your father's packing shed got picked up for public drunkenness."

"Which does happen every now and then," she put in.

"Exactly, and no one blames the company. But the growers, not to mention the Teamsters, are itching for a way to discredit us. They've been claiming all along that the UFW isn't really a labor union but just a mob of malcontents who want to destroy the 'American Way of Life.' What could play more into their hands?"

"Judy's father was over here last night. It's crazy—he's crazy. He insists the UFW is to blame for Judy's using drugs. He actually threatened to 'get' the union for hurting her. I mean, he was positively irrational."

"And some all too rational people are more than willing to use his rage." Philip paused, but Holly could find no words to reassure him. "Well," he said, "I have to go. There's another meeting tonight."

"Watch out, Philip." She couldn't find the words to share her premonition with him, but she felt she had to warn him, somehow. "Judy's father . . ."

"He was just upset, Holly. I don't think he'll follow through on those threats. And if it will ease your mind, we're not meeting at union headquarters. We're meeting here, at my folks' place, so nobody will even know it's a union meeting."

"I'm glad."

"Holly, sometimes I wish I weren't involved in this."

"You don't really mean that. You have to be part of it. You believe in it."

"I guess you're right. I never could duck out on a fight. But sometime, when the dust dies down, can we go back to the beach and watch the sunset again?"

"We will," she vowed. "And I pray it will be soon. Good night, Philip."

"Good night, and God bless."

Holly was exhausted. She went to bed early, but she was awakened before dawn by the strident ring of the phone. Her father was in the hallway in his robe. His face was red, his mouth hard with anger. "That fool!

That stupid, stubborn idiot." He hung up and turned to his daughter.

"Daddy, what's happened?"

"That was Sam. There's been . . ." His voice dropped. "Holly, somebody firebombed the DeLaCruz home last night."

"Philip!"

"I don't know," he said gently. "Sam says there was a union meeting there last night."

She nodded, her fear enveloping her.

"Somebody . . . Sam says he doesn't know who, but from the tone of his voice, I'm afraid he knows more than he's admitting—anyhow, someone threw a bomb through a front window. They thought Chavez was there, he says. That's who they were after."

"But was anyone hurt, Daddy?" *Please, God, not Philip.*

"Sam said somebody was killed. He didn't know who. Several people were shaken up, but he said one man was dead."

"Oh, God, don't let it be Philip," she prayed. Ellen joined them, and Ron told her what Sam had said. The two women waited as Ron turned the dial searching for local news.

". . . elderly Filipino man, who was not injured by the bomb but apparently died from heart failure at the scene," they heard an announcer say. *Elderly. Not Philip then.* The radio droned on. "The sheriff's department says there are no suspects yet, though they surmise the incident was connected with the ongoing farm labor dispute. Most of the people in the house at the time were known associates of Cesar Chavez, including the dead man's son, Philip DeLaCruz."

The knot of fear dropped from Holly's throat to her stomach. "Julio." She felt her mother gently place a hand over her own. The announcer went on to other news.

"I have to call them," Holly said. An unfamiliar accent answered after several rings. "The family is grief-stricken and does not wish to talk to anyone." Her ear rang with the resounding clatter of the receiver at the other end of the line.

A wild, incoherent Judy called before Holly left for work. "How could you, Holly?" she screamed. "When you turned us in to the sheriff, I tried to tell myself you meant well. You had no right, but at least I could believe you were trying to save me from myself."

"Judy." Holly struggled to plead her innocence, but Judy wasn't listening.

"You self-righteous hypocrite! You're just jealous because you haven't got the nerve to live your own life, and you can't let me live mine. I thought you'd be satisfied with taking Vic away from me. And my baby!" Judy's wail hurt Holly's ears as the words tore her heart.

"Judy, listen," she protested once more, but again Judy refused to hear her.

"You really had me fooled about Philip. I actually thought you were falling in love with him."

Holly's eyes brimmed. "I am," she whispered, but the words were lost in Judy's tirade.

"The worst of it is that you had him believing it too. You used him, made him trust you, and all the time you were spying for my father and his farmers' association."

"I never . . ."

"I suppose you're going to tell me you never meant for anyone to get killed. Well, somebody did. And you're going to pay." Holly thought Judy's scream could be heard all over the house, and, in fact, her mother did come into the hallway as Judy concluded. "We'll get you for this, all of you." The receiver at the other end of the line crashed down.

Holly answered her mother's unspoken question. "That was Judy, Mom. She's . . . She just wasn't making any sense. She must still be on drugs."

For the next three days, Holly tried over and over to reach Philip, or even Cici, but the answer remained the same. "The family does not wish to be disturbed." She left messages of condolence: trite, meaningless words trying to convey her sorrow. There was no response.

"It's so unfair," Holly sobbed to her mother as they drove from Salinas to Soledad. She was grateful that her mother had insisted on going to Julio DeLaCruz's funeral with her. "Why Julio? He wasn't even a member of the union, let alone a leader. He owned his own farm and farmed his own land. He didn't even hire migrant labor."

"It could as easily have been Philip," her mother reminded her.

"It could have been," Holly agreed, grateful, in spite of herself, that he had been spared. "Philip didn't have to be involved, either. It wasn't their fight." Holly thought of Philip's dark eyes, glowing as he talked of the hopes that rested with the UFW. "It's what he is, Mother. He just has to fight for what he believes is right."

They turned off the freeway onto the drab back streets of Soledad. The dusty parking lot of Our Lady of Solitude Catholic Church was already filled, and Holly pulled onto a gravelly shoulder in the next block. She saw Paul and Marianne across the narrow lane and joined them.

"Judy isn't with you?" Ellen queried.

Marianne sighed as Paul told them that Judy had left the house two days before.

"She flew into a rage when she heard the news about Julio," Marianne explained. "She said some awful things about, well, about how you had betrayed them all, Holly, and about her father. She's so mixed up. She seems to be blaming you for this too—you and her father."

"I know," Holly told her. "She called me the morning after Julio was killed. She must have been high. She didn't make any sense. She accused me of being a spy, of using Philip." She bit her lip, and Marianne squeezed her hand. "I wouldn't; I couldn't," she vowed as they walked along the curbless, crumbling pavement.

Paul stopped as they neared the church entrance. "Many of the people here will think of us as outsiders," he warned. "Maybe even as the enemy."

"You and Marianne? You've been working day and night at their clinic."

"Had been," he said sadly. "We've been replaced. It was 'suggested' that a Hispanic doctor might be 'more acceptable.' I expect they won't want Holly back in the lab either."

"Lots of growers already think of the UFW more as a civil rights movement than a union," Ellen pointed out. "Won't that attitude only estrange us more?"

"It's late," Marianne reminded them. "We'd better go in."

"Yes," her husband agreed. "But sit near the back. We are here to pay our respects to a good man, not to intrude on the grief of his people."

Holly scanned the backs of heads and was grateful to recognize Judy's carrot-colored locks in one corner. *At least she hasn't left the valley.*

Holly spotted Julio's family in a front pew. *Cici was so proud of Julio, so devoted to him. Could it really have been love that brought her here twenty-six years ago, to a strange land, with a man nearly twice her age? Well, if it wasn't love then, it became love.*

Philip sat next to his mother, head bowed. John, home from his freshman year at Berkeley, had taken his place on Cici's other side, and Holly guessed that the young man beyond him was the third brother. Angela sat next to Philip, and a young couple she didn't know, the other sister and her husband, probably, filled the pew. Holly thought of her own father. *How lost and alone they must feel.*

A surprised murmur swept the little church, and Holly realized that the small, inconspicuous man who stepped forward to deliver the eulogy was Cesar Chavez. He spoke softly, but his words carried easily to the far corners of the building. Every other sound ceased when he began to speak. *Mesmerizing* was the word Holly found to describe his voice, *like Philip's*, she thought. And she knew he spoke the truth when he told them a martyr had been made in Soledad.

The funeral mass ended, and Holly edged her way

through the crowd toward Cici and Philip. Cici's swollen eyes were brooding black set in dark purple circles. She saw Holly and turned away.

Philip saw her too. He stared, as if he were surprised to see her there. *Surely he knew I would come*, she thought. She began to make her way past the clustered mourners.

He started to follow his mother, then turned and roughly pushed his way toward her. His eyes, too, were swollen from weeping, but they still glowed, burning into her heart as he faced her. "Why did you come?" he asked, but he didn't pause for an answer. "Did you come to gloat? Don't. Cesar was right. Now we have a martyr, and we shall win. My father's death will not be wasted."

"Philip!"

He was gone, back among the milling crowd, before she could protest his bitter words.

Chapter Seventeen

*B*ecause of her baby, Judy went back to the Hanlon homestead after a few days. With her there, Holly found it awkward to visit her Grandma Carrie, so she welcomed Marianne's phone call. "We have to be in San Francisco for the weekend," Marianne explained, "and we thought we'd take Judy and the baby with us, so they can visit Vic's parents. You know we don't like to leave Mother alone too much, at her age. Could you just drive down and see that she gets a good Sunday dinner?"

When Holly arrived at the farm, Carrie welcomed her with a warm smile, though she protested firmly the idea that she needed someone to look in on her. "I'm not as fast as I used to be," she admitted, "but I can still find my way around my own kitchen."

She proved it by making stuffed pork chops for them. They talked about the latest news over the chops. "Putting Chavez in jail for contempt of court," Carrie snorted. "Best way I can think of to drum up sympathy for his boycott."

Holly agreed as she began to slice the warm apple pie. "How do you like having a baby in the house after all these years?" she asked.

"She's the best baby, Holly. No trouble at all." Carrie shook her head. "Judy insists she's going to leave here as soon as her probation is over and find that man, Vic. If only he'd settle down and marry her."

"Vic? Not likely, Grandma."

"Well, I can hope, and pray. And how about you? How is your life going?"

"Oh, just fine. I love my job."

"I think it's wonderful that girls can get good educations now and do so many interesting things. When I was a girl . . ." She looked away, and Holly knew she was remembering. "I was a shop girl, and that was pretty awful. Then I learned typewriting, which was considered quite daring. Of course two of my girls became nurses. I've always been proud of them."

"I like the challenge of working in the lab. Nursing's still a good profession, but, well, I never thought I had the 'people skills' for it. I like doing my bit behind the scenes."

Holly began clearing the table. "Forget the dishes for now," Carrie said, "and sit down again and tell me what's really going on."

"What do you mean, Grandma? Nothing's 'going on' as you put it."

"That's what I mean. There was another young man, wasn't there, after Greg? Last time you were here I got the idea you were quite taken with him."

"Oh, it wasn't anything, really. He . . . We . . ."

"Marianne told me his father was the one who was killed in that bombing. And Judy seems to think her father had something to do with it." She shook her head. "Sam McLean has a bit of his grandfather's temper, but he's no more a killer than I am."

"I hope you're right."

"Anyhow, that's got nothing to do with you and your young man. You're going to put up a fight for him, aren't you?"

"Grandma!"

"Don't tell me in this day of liberated women the idea shocks you." Carrie laughed. "Why, way back in 1900 women fought for their men."

Holly sat down again. "Grandma, he isn't 'my man.' Maybe, if his father hadn't been killed . . ."

Carrie patted Holly's hand as if she were still a little girl. "Talking things out helps sometimes. I may be an old lady, but I'm still a good listener."

Holly's eyes began to burn with unshed tears. *Grandma's ninety years old. How could she understand how I feel?* "I don't know what might have happened between us if things had been different," she said. "All I know is that I miss him. I miss him terribly."

"Tell me about him, what he's like."

A teardrop slipped out. "Maybe it would help to talk to you about it," she admitted. "I can't talk to Mom. She's just relieved that it's over. She was afraid I'd be hurt because of the difference in our backgrounds and everything. She always hoped I'd get back together with Greg."

"Yes, like she did with Ron. But that isn't going to happen, is it?"

"He started dating a girl from the lab the week after I broke up with him. And they're perfect for each other." She laughed. "You might even say they deserve each other. No, I have no regrets."

"But you said you broke up with Greg because you realized you weren't really in love with him. You must have felt something for him once."

"He was practically the only boy I ever dated, Grandma. Most of the boys in high school didn't pay that much attention to me." She paused thoughtfully. "I always figured I just wasn't the popular type, but I wonder, now, if it wasn't more that they all thought of me as Greg's girl."

"You were apart for the better part of two years, and you never broke it off then."

Holly wondered what Carrie was driving at. "I guess it was easier to go along," she said, finally. "I don't think I ever expected to fall in love the way other girls did—over and over again." She chuckled. "Or head over heels, like the girls in romance novels."

Her grandmother's silence spoke volumes. *I broke off with Greg after I met Philip—after I fell in love with Philip.* "Am I being an utter fool?" Holly asked. "Philip and I only dated a half dozen times; it was only a few weeks."

"From what Marianne has told me, he's a devout Christian, loyal to his family, dedicated to doing good."

"I know he's a good man, but so is Greg."

"But you weren't in love with Greg."

"And am I, with Philip?" she mused. "I never believed in love at first sight. And, besides, he's so, well, so

150

intense, and involved. I never quite thought of myself as a zealot, you know." She chuckled. "That's Marianne, not me."

"Your mother, too, at least when she was your age."

"Yes, it's funny, isn't it? She's so conservative now. But I've wondered sometimes what was wrong with me," Holly mused. "I guess I'm behind the times; I'm more like the 'me' generation of the '50s than like my contemporaries. It isn't that I don't care. I want to do the right things; help people; be a useful citizen. But activism turns me off."

"And no wonder, in this day. Such awful things go on now in the name of justice."

"And Judy got caught up in it. She started out with good intentions. I know she did. But it all got mixed up with free love and drugs and . . ."

"And Vic Bigelow?" Carrie queried. "Judy made some bad choices, and Vic was one of them."

"She thinks she's in love with him. But how can that be love?"

Carrie didn't answer the question. "Holly," she said softly, "you can't confuse Philip DeLaCruz with Vic Bigelow."

"Of course not!" *But,* Holly couldn't help recalling, *Judy had insisted Vic was different too.* "Philip meant a lot to me," she admitted. "He challenged me. He made me face myself and my life. He showed me the world beyond my world: poor people, hungry right here in this valley I've always thought of as rich; sick people without money to pay doctors. And he showed me the others, too—the ones who aren't poor, but just different."

Carrie nodded as Holly continued. "His own family.

151

Do you know how they came here? How the men came to work the fields? Some of them still do, after forty years! A lot of them were in the army and brought home war brides. They came back and bought homes and started families right after World War II, just like my folks and Sam and Aunt Liz. But I never even knew they existed."

"They don't sound so different from us, Holly. Your Grandpa Matt came here as a farmhand too."

Holly remembered the happy evening with the De-LaCruz family. "They were so open, so warm at first," she told Carrie. "They made me feel welcome then. Now Cici scarcely speaks to me. And Philip—Philip hates me. I don't understand why, but he hates me."

Holly picked up the dinner dishes then, and Carrie followed her into the kitchen. "And Judy hates me too," Holly sighed, as she drew the dish water.

"Judy's still not thinking clearly. One of these days she'll realize you're the same good friend you've always been to her."

"Maybe."

She saw Philip now and then. Salinas was small. His apartment, like her home, was near the college. His mother worked with her. It was inevitable that they would run into each other.

It was an evening in early December. A winter storm had blown in from the Gulf of Alaska bringing heavy, cold rain that moved quickly inland. The air was clean and brisk. Christmas lights reflected brightly in the puddles. Holly had always loved Christmas shopping, until this year. *Maybe*, she told herself, *if I can just get myself started, I'll get in the mood.*

She was in the little Christian bookstore, looking for some records for Judy. *Not too overtly Christian, but still, a message. Maybe just Christmas music. She'd be more likely to listen to that, and yet nothing teaches the gospel more clearly than the simple folk carols and hymns of Christmas.*

She jumped when she realized Philip was standing in front of her in the long line leading to the cash register. *He hasn't seen me. Do I dare say anything?* "Hello, Philip. How are you?" She more than half-hoped he could hear the burning desire beneath the trite words.

He turned quickly, startled by her voice, and his dark eyes flashed. His lips parted, but no words came. He turned away, seemingly intent on the children's books in a nearby rack.

"Philip, please? I'm sorry about Chavez being in jail," she offered tentatively, afraid to bring up the personal tragedy that had driven them apart.

"Don't be. That contempt charge is just what the boycott needed," he responded brusquely. "Just look at the press we got when Ethel Kennedy prayed at that portable shrine outside the Salinas jail. That's worth more for our cause than pickets in every Safeway parking lot in the country."

At least he's acknowledging my presence. She pressed her luck. "Yes, it probably does help the boycott," she offered, "but it must be very hard for Cesar and his family."

"They expected it." The coldness was still there, in his dark eyes, as he turned to pay for his purchases. "But I forgot. You people don't understand about martyrs." He left the bookstore without another word.

She rushed through her own transaction and hurried outside, sure he would be long gone, yet hoping he had waited. She saw his familiar pickup parked between the store and her car. He slouched behind the wheel, face buried in his hands. *He does care.*

She started toward him, then hesitated. *What will I say?* As she pondered, she heard the purr of the truck engine. She saw the pain on his face as he looked at her, and then quickly away. He pulled out into the street and was gone.

Knowing that Philip was hurting as much as she was might have given Holly hope but for the bitterness of his words. To escape the memory of them she poured herself into the mechanics of celebrating Christmas—shopping, wrapping, the Sunday school program.

On Christmas Day, as always, the family gathered at Grandma Carrie's. The farm profits might have been smaller than usual, but the pile of gifts under the big tree in the parlor belied any talk of hardship.

Judy was there, still edgy, but less thin. Her probation was almost over. "Another month," she snarled to Holly. "Another couple of months, and I'm taking my baby and getting out of here." She fled upstairs, refusing to join the family gathering that included her father.

She let Marianne bring the baby down briefly, and Sam's eyes watered as he bounced the little girl on his knee. "It could have been so different," he mourned. "Why couldn't he at least have married her when he found out she was pregnant and settled down with a decent job? But no. He went out and got himself arrested for dealing drugs. Didn't he even care what happened to his own child?"

The baby began to cry, and Marianne started to pick her up. "Let me take her upstairs," Holly offered. "Maybe I can persuade Judy to come down."

"I doubt it," Marianne told her, as she handed the baby to Holly. "But do try. It's Christmas."

Holly tapped lightly on the bedroom door. "Carrie seems to need her mommy," she said softly.

Judy opened the door and took her child in her arms. "Sounds like she's wet," she observed.

"Please, may I come in, Judy?" Holly asked. "You know, you've never heard my side of the story. Don't you owe me that after so many years of friendship?"

"So many years? You haven't really been my friend since—well, since Vic anyhow."

"I wanted to be. I still do."

"Sure. You figured as long as Vic was in jail he was away from me." Judy laid the baby on the bed and reached for a clean diaper. "You'd do anything to keep Vic and me apart, wouldn't you? You know, I used to think you were jealous."

"Jealous?" Holly was incredulous. "Of Vic?"

"Yeah. Greg was such a square." She laughed harshly. "How could any girl think she was in love with a nothing like that? But why now, when you could have had someone like Philip? Holly . . ."

Tears welled in her eyes. "I've lost Philip," she whispered.

"Oh, so you're sorry now." Judy threw the words at her. "I still can't understand how you could do it, you know. I could believe you turned me in because you thought you were saving me from myself. But how could you betray Philip? He was in love with you. I even thought you were in love with him."

"Please believe me," Holly insisted. "Please. I didn't call the sheriff's office about the drugs. And as for betraying Philip, for being any part of his father's death . . ." She reached out to her cousin, taking Judy's baby powder-covered hands in her own. "Judy, how could you even think such a thing? How could such a story even get started?" *And how could Philip believe it?* she added silently.

She thought she saw a tear fall as Judy pinned the last corner of Carrie's diaper. "You were the only one outside of the union who knew about that meeting, Holly. You were the only one who could have told my father that Chavez was going to be in that house that night."

"Me?" Holly tried to recall the events preceding Julio's death. "How would I have known?"

"Don't bother to play innocent. Philip remembers. He told you, when he called to cancel your date." She tucked the baby into her crib. "And everybody knows about my father's threats."

"Your father had nothing against Philip, Judy. The union, maybe, but not Philip and certainly not Julio."

"He knew Philip was close to Cesar. And he knew Philip and I knew each other too. Oh, I don't believe my father wanted anyone to get killed, or you, either. But when you throw firebombs, people do get hurt. And you're as much to blame as my father is."

Holly opened her mouth to protest her innocence, but Judy pushed her toward the door. "And don't make it worse by lying about it." The door snapped closed between them, and Holly brushed tears from her eyes as she slowly descended the staircase.

Harry McLean's son, Dave, was talking when she entered the living room. He had come up for Christmas from the Imperial Valley where he managed the family's southern California holdings. "Too bad things couldn't have gone here the way they did down there," he was saying. "The UFW organizers held a few meetings in town and passed out their cards. No violence; hardly any trouble at all."

"Chavez and his hotheads were all up here," Bob commented.

"Yes, and so were the Teamsters, and your 'farmers association,'" Dave reminded them.

"You think we should sign, don't you?" Ted asked him.

"Yes, I do," Dave answered without hesitation. "This spring, when the workers come back, before things have time to get out of hand again, I think you should open your fields to the organizers and let them talk to your workers. And if the workers join them, yes, give them a fair contract. It's the only way to do business, in the long run, and it will be a lot less painful if we do it before we're pressured anymore."

Holly wasn't surprised at the nods of agreement from her parents, from Marianne and Paul, from Uncle Harry even. What did surprise her, and everyone else at the table, were the words from Sam McLean. "Yes," he said reluctantly but firmly. "Yes. We should talk to them."

What changed his mind? Holly wondered. She feared she knew the answer. *He feels guilty, doesn't he? And he wants to undo the wrong.*

"There's been too much trouble already," Sam concluded. "It's time to make peace."

Grandma Carrie's whispered "Praise God" echoed around the room.

157

Chapter Eighteen

Cici, we need to talk," Holly pleaded. "Please. It's a new year, and we have to clear out the garbage of the old. I know it's been awful for you, but there has been a terrible misunderstanding. Can't we please go out to lunch somewhere?"

Cici's smile had vanished in October and not returned. She turned somber eyes to Holly. "Do we really have anything to say to each other?"

"I have a lot to say to you," Holly insisted. "I know what you think, but you're wrong. Don't I have a right to tell you how much I'm hurting, too, and that, no matter what you've heard, I had nothing to do with what happened?"

Cici wordlessly slipped out of her lab coat and into a heavy sweater.

"Please, Cici. I thought we were friends. Can you forget that because of some rumor?"

"I don't want to believe it, but everything adds up."

Cici studied her face, and sighed. "All right. I should at least hear you out."

They ordered hamburgers to eat in Holly's car, but neither of them was very hungry. "Cici," Holly began tentatively, "I never really got to know your husband, but I wanted to. I know how much you loved him. He shouldn't have been hurt by this; he wasn't even involved, really."

"No one thinks you meant him dead," Cici said bitterly. "Even Sam McLean didn't want that—Cesar maybe, but not Julio. But when such hate is released . . ."

"Cici, I honestly don't know whether Sam had anything to do with it. But he was angry, senselessly angry, about what had happened to Judy."

"And what did that have to do with the union, let alone with Julio?"

"Nothing, nothing at all, and I guess that's why I can't really believe he had anything to do with the bombing. But even if he did, I didn't."

"Then how did he find out about the meeting?"

"I don't know," Holly insisted. "I don't know who threw the bomb, and I have no idea how they knew about the meeting, or even if they knew."

"If?" Cici questioned harshly.

"Lots of people knew Philip was working with Chavez, and there has been so much violence these past months—at UFW homes, and at growers' homes too. Why are you so sure this was different?"

"We know who threw the bomb, Holly. Philip recognized him. And people saw him with your cousin that day."

JEAN GRANT

"Cici, if that's so, why hasn't he been arrested?" *Philip knows who it was! But they kept saying on TV and in the papers that there were no clues.*

"Why is no one ever arrested? You said yourself there have been dozens of such incidents, but the sheriff always says he doesn't have enough evidence."

"Someone died this time, Cici. If Philip recognized the man, if there was an eyewitness . . ."

"He told them what he saw. Nothing happened."

Holly could scarcely believe the bitter words. "Then you should go to the district attorney, or even to the newspapers if you have to. Cici, no one must be allowed to get away with murder."

"Murder? An old man had a heart attack." Cici shrugged, though her eyes had filled with tears.

"Murder," Holly insisted. "If you know who did it you have to demand an investigation."

Cici studied Holly's face, puzzled. "You mean it, don't you?" she said. "You feel the same helplessness we feel."

"Yes, I do. Can you please believe that I wasn't involved?"

"Holly, Philip remembers telling you about the union meeting," Cici told her. "But there must have been others who knew. I guess you wouldn't want an investigation if you were afraid of what it might reveal."

Holly grasped the offered hand. "I am afraid, Cici, but for Sam, not for myself. How can we find out the truth?"

"I believe you've told me the truth about the fire. I hate to ask you this, but have you told the truth about

160

the drug raid too? Judy McLean is sure it was you who called the sheriff."

Holly shook her head. "I thought about doing it—to help her straighten out. And I talked to my Aunt Marianne about it. We think someone at the clinic overheard us. But Marianne convinced me I shouldn't say anything—that it would be better to go slow and to trust God to draw Judy away from them."

"That is probably where the story started. You were overheard, and when the raid occurred the wrong conclusion was drawn. But Judy hates you because of it." Cici shook her head sadly. "It may have been Judy who suggested you were spying for her father."

To keep me from Philip as she thought I had taken Vic from her? Holly didn't want to believe it, but Judy had been acting irrationally. *Maybe.* "Thank you for listening to me, Cici, and for trusting me. I guess the next step is to try to talk to Judy."

They drove back to the hospital. As Cici opened the car door she spoke once more. "I do believe you, Holly. And I will tell Philip I believe you."

Holly drove down to Soledad after work that day. Judy was still living in Grandma Carrie's old farmhouse with Paul and Marianne. Or at least she was using a bedroom there. "She even eats in her room," Marianne told Holly. "She scarcely speaks to us. I think she's off the drugs though, unless someone's sneaking her a supply."

"Could they do that, right here under your nose?"

"We aren't her jailers," Marianne pointed out. "She comes and goes. Even if we could watch her every minute, would that help? We have tried to show her trust. Otherwise, how can she prove herself trustworthy?"

"I hope you're right."

"We have to be, or there is no hope for her. Her probation ends in March. If she wants to go, then, and take little Carrie with her, we can't stop her. So we're trying to make her want to stay, for her own sake and for the baby's."

"Marianne, I need to talk to her."

"I doubt she'll listen. She's still sure you turned them in to the police."

"I know, and I didn't. But it isn't just that anymore. I finally talked to Cici DeLaCruz."

"Oh, I'm so glad. Did you convince her you had nothing to do with what happened?"

Holly nodded. "She says Philip recognized the man who threw the bomb, but the police refused to take any action. Can you believe that?"

"I guess it depends on who it was. Surely you realize the police haven't been entirely impartial lately."

"But to let someone get away with murder?"

"Try to see it from the sheriff's viewpoint, Holly. Philip said he recognized the arsonist; the arsonist had an alibi. The sheriff knows the suspect, probably, or the person who provided the alibi anyway. So who does he believe?"

"They had an obligation to investigate."

"You'd think so. Yes, I think so too. But the sheriff didn't think so. Besides, it wasn't murder, technically. Julio wasn't injured in the fire but died of a heart attack. Anyhow, what does all that have to do with Judy?" Marianne asked.

"Cici thinks Judy may have started the rumor about my spying for her father."

"That's ridiculous. Judy knows you too well to think you'd do that. Even if she could believe you would betray her, she has to think your intentions were good. But that you would date Philip so you could report his actions to Sam? Besides, Judy knows you too well not to know how you felt about Philip."

"Was it really that obvious?" Holly blinked back tears.

"It still is," Marianne observed, hugging her close.

"But isn't it just as bad for me to accuse Judy of turning Philip against me as for her to blame me for putting Vic in prison?" Holly paused. "I came down here today to confront her. You don't think I should, do you?"

"I don't know. Something was growing between you and Philip, something good. You want that relationship back."

"But can that ever be? He was quick enough to believe the worst, after all."

"His father had just died, Holly. His mother has come around. Why shouldn't he?"

A flicker of hope stirred in her. "If he wants to."

Marianne nodded. "If he wants to believe in you, he will see that the gossip is meaningless."

"So it doesn't really matter who started the rumor, does it?"

"No, and if you confront Judy I'm afraid you'll only drive her farther away. Talk to her if you want to. Tell her again that you weren't the anonymous caller, if you must. But . . ."

"You're right, as usual." Holly returned the hug. "I'll

just go up and try for a friendly reconciliation. Say a prayer that she'll listen, though."

"And that Philip will listen too?" Marianne asked, smiling.

"I tried to talk to Judy last night," Holly told Cici the next morning, "but she's still so bitter. The important thing right now is for me to win back her trust. If I accused her of lying about me, I'd only drive her farther away."

"She might have evidence, though—evidence enough for the police."

"I doubt it. I can't believe she would deliberately lie in order to implicate me. Not even if she was high; no matter how angry she was with me. If she started that story, she believed it—wrongly—but she must have believed it was true."

"Just her admission that she was the source might be enough to clear you, though."

"With whom?" *With Philip*, her heart told her, *but Philip has to believe me for my own sake, not because someone clears my name.* "Cici, you believe me. Judy won't change her mind about the drug raid just because I confront her on the bombing. And . . ."

She couldn't bring herself to say aloud the one name that mattered. Cici said the words Holly was thinking. "Philip shouldn't need her confession, Holly. I don't think he does, anymore. But he loved his father, and the death was so senseless. He needed some reason, some focus for his hurt. And you were there."

"I cared for him. You knew that, didn't you? And I thought he cared for me."

"He did. Holly, I never saw him with another girl like he was with you. Maybe that's why he was so quick to blame you—because he had hoped too much and couldn't trust his hopes."

Holly was grateful that the noisy slosh of the pipette washer covered their words as Kathy walked into the utility room. "Oops. Am I interrupting something?" she asked, though it should have been obvious that she was. "Just wanted to tell both of you the good news." She flashed her left hand, and Holly gasped as she saw the sparkling solitaire. "Yup, Greg. Hey, I hope you're okay with this, Holly. I know you two went together for years, but, well, we just seemed to click."

"I think it's wonderful. Congratulations, Kathy." She meant it, she realized, though the announcement coming this soon astonished her. *Greg needs to get on with his life, and Kathy and he are a good match.*

Kathy breezed on through the utility room to spread her news, and Cici turned back to Holly. "Philip knows he was wrong, Holly. He just doesn't know how to tell you so."

Chapter Nineteen

*I*t was another accidental en-
counter, at the supermarket
this time. Holly saw Philip first as he waited in the
checkout line. She hesitated, remembering Cici's words
but not quite believing them, then wheeled her cart to
the end of the next line. While she wanted to speak, the
thought of another bitter rebuff held her back.

"Hello, Holly," he said, the timbre of his soft voice
carrying through the chatter around them. "How are you?"

Cici has talked to him. Holly was trembling. *Be noncha-
lant,* she told herself. *Well, try to be.* "Oh, I'm just fine."
Now. "And you? Are your classes keeping you busy?"

"Pretty much."

She felt his eyes on her, and his look still stirred her
as it had that first July afternoon. *Is he searching for words
just as I am?* "Your mother tells me you've finished your
dissertation," she said.

"Yes. I'll be meeting with my committee at Davis
very soon, and if all goes well I'll be Doctor DeLaCruz in

June." Her heart thumped with hope as he smiled a crooked little half-smile at her. "I don't quite believe it."

"Why not? You've worked hard for it." *Does that mean he'll be going to South America soon?* she wondered, frightened suddenly that time might rob her of the hope that was coming back to her.

She wanted to ask, but the checker had totaled his order. He picked up the bag of groceries. "Maybe I'll see you again sometime," he said.

"I hope so." She could only pray, as he walked away, that he heard her words and believed them.

Kathy's chatter had always fluttered in and out of Holly's consciousness as they worked together in the lab. *It's like a soap opera,* Holly told herself. *It doesn't matter if you miss a few days. Anything important will come around again.*

Now Kathy was full of plans for her June wedding. "It's only a couple of months," she was saying, again, "and I've got a jillion things to do."

Holly tried to listen over the whirr of the centrifuge. "Mmmm," she grunted.

"Look, if it makes you uncomfortable, my talking about Greg . . ."

"It doesn't," Holly insisted. "I've told you over and over that I broke off with Greg because I simply wasn't in love with him. I'm glad you're together; really I am."

"But you'd started seeing Philip by then, hadn't you?"

Kathy was getting uncomfortably close to the truth. Holly took her sample tubes out of the centrifuge and turned away.

"Say," Kathy persisted, "there are several good-looking teachers at the college. Maybe we could fix you up with somebody—a double date, Saturday?"

Holly's cheeks flushed. "No thanks," she snapped. "As a matter of fact, I have a date for Saturday." Kathy shrugged and walked away. Holly took a handful of pipettes from the drawer Cici was filling and began setting up the morning's run of blood sugar tests.

Cici looked up, surprised. "A date?"

"Okay, so I lied," Holly whispered. "I just . . ."

"I see." Cici smiled in understanding. "Then how would you like to have supper with me? My kids are all going to be away this weekend, and I'll be lonesome."

Holly returned the smile. "I just couldn't face a double date with Kathy and Greg and some 'good looking teacher.'"

"I thought so. You're really not a very good liar, are you? So, how about Saturday?"

Holly had to admit that she was a little disappointed to find only Cici's car in the long driveway that led through the neatly tended strawberry fields. She had half hoped that Philip would just "happen" to be there, for all Cici had told her she'd be alone.

The low, sprawling house had not been repainted yet, she realized. The new patch in the stucco near the door was an ugly gray. Soot stains spread out from the patch, fuzzy, black fingers that intruded into the pale pink of the old paint. Holly tried not to look at the obvious reminder of Cici's tragedy. She blinked back tears as she knocked on the new front door.

Cici welcomed her in and led the way to the kitchen. "We haven't finished redecorating," she explained.

"Philip and the kids have worked so hard, but by the time we had the wall rebuilt it was time to set out the new berry plants. And then Philip had to study for his exams."

"When are his orals? It must be soon."

"Oh, they're all over. It's official now. He will receive his doctorate in June."

"You must be so proud of him."

Cici brushed a tear from her eye. "So proud. If only his father could see . . . Julio was always so proud of Philip—of all our children."

Holly followed Cici into the dining room where she set two places opposite each other near the head of the long table. Cici gestured toward the living room, draped with drop cloths. "Philip was going to paint this weekend, but he had to go out of town."

Holly tried to hide her disappointment. "Union business?" she queried.

"No. He hasn't much to do with the union anymore."

"After what happened . . ."

"They didn't scare him off, Holly. Never that. But the UFW is part of the AFL-CIO now and has a professional staff. They don't need him that much anymore." She forced a laugh. "No, Philip's off looking for another crusade. Did he ever tell you about that crazy idea he has of going to South America as a missionary?"

So he hasn't given up the idea. "He mentioned it once or twice, but I thought now . . ." Holly's eyes swept the nearly empty room.

"I would never hold him back. I can manage. My second son graduates from Cal in June and expects to come back here to teach. I have my job, and it pays enough for my immediate needs. Angela and John may have to work their way through college, but Philip did." The proud half-smile came back. "It didn't hurt him."

"But you can't take care of the farm, can you?"

"I can sell it. It's good land. In fact, I could probably get enough out of it to buy a little place in town and still help the youngest with their college expenses." She directed a determined gaze to Holly. "I am not a destitute widow. Philip is totally free to live his own life."

"I didn't mean . . ." *Does she mean he's free to get married? As if that were the barrier between us!* "You know how it is. We all get these ideas sometimes about going off to change the world. He said something about working with a mission group, teaching modern agricultural methods in an underdeveloped area like the altiplano."

"He went to L.A. today for an interview," Cici told her. "I probably shouldn't admit it, and don't you ever tell Philip I said so, but I do sincerely pray it doesn't happen."

Holly couldn't keep from returning the conspiratorial smile. "And after all you just said about letting him live his own life."

"His own life, yes. The lives of a lot of poor Indians in South America, no. I'm not selfish for myself. But I'm terribly selfish for my children. Philip's worked so hard, and he could have such a brilliant future right here. He could teach at any college, even at the university. He could work for the government in the Department of Agriculture. He could even go into politics himself someday. My son, the president."

Holly laughed, and Cici laughed with her. "But you're right," Holly said. "Philip could do a great deal of good right here in the Salinas Valley."

They washed the dishes together. At Holly's insistence Cici carefully wrote out recipes for the mouth-watering chicken adobo and spicy lumpia Holly assured her she was going to learn to make. "Though now that I'm getting an idea of how much work is involved, I suspect I won't do it very often."

"Maybe you should just come and visit me when you get hungry for Filipino cooking," Cici told her as they heard the sound of a car in the gravel. Cici jumped, and Holly, too, stopped to listen, both recalling another night when an unexpected car had driven up that driveway.

The door rattled, and they both laughed nervously as a familiar voice called out "Mama? Are you still up?"

"In the kitchen, Philip. I didn't expect you back until tomorrow. I have company."

Philip seemed startled to find Holly in his mother's kitchen. He stared, briefly, and then turned deliberately away. "The interview was over fairly early, and I decided to save a night's motel bill," he explained.

"I told Holly you were in L.A. talking to some people about going to South America. Did it go well?"

"That depends." He seemed uneasy.

I should go home, Holly told herself. *He doesn't want me here.*

But Cici had placed herself in the doorway as she questioned her son. "Don't keep us in suspense. Are you going or not?"

"Not right away." He fidgeted, but Cici didn't move. He glanced at Holly, who stared at the floor. "They want to go ahead with their demonstration farm and educational project in Bolivia, and they told me I seemed right for the project. But they don't have the funds yet. They won't be able to make a decision for several months."

Several months. Holly hoped her relief didn't show. *There's still time.*

"Don't you think that's best, Philip?" Cici asked innocently. "That gives you more time to think about it and be sure this is really what you want to do."

"I'm sure now, Mama. But it is better timing. By then you'll have this place sold and be settled in town."

Cici nodded. "Yes. It will be easier to lose you by then, if you're still sure about going." She stepped back from the doorway. "Thanks for stopping by to tell me."

Holly followed her out of the kitchen. "It's late," she stammered. "It's been a very pleasant evening, but I should be going home."

"Nonsense! It's early, and besides I really did want to talk to you about what you said last week." Cici turned to her son. "Philip, Holly thinks you should talk to the district attorney about what you told the sheriff after the firebomb."

"What makes you think he would do any more about it than the sheriff did?" he asked, directing his eyes past Holly to his mother. "I told him I saw the man clearly and recognized him. But he claims he was playing poker with several prominent people. It's his word, and theirs, against mine. Holly may not know what that means, but you do, Mama."

"How can you be so sure he wouldn't listen?" Holly protested. "Why do you have to believe everyone is against you?" The angry words slipped out before she thought about them. She started to apologize, but Cici interrupted.

"The district attorney might listen, Philip, and investigate at least. Maybe the alibi wouldn't stand up if someone asked the right people the right questions."

"If not, you have friends in the press, you know,"

Holly interrupted. "Surely you could find someone who would look into it further."

He really looked at her then, for the first time in months. "So what Mama said is true. You really aren't afraid of an investigation, are you?"

"I am afraid, Philip. I don't know what they might find out. It might hurt someone I care about. But then, it might clear him too."

"And you?" He said it very softly, longingly.

"I was astonished by your words at your father's funeral. I know, now, about the rumors. But they aren't true. Believe me, Philip, I didn't . . ."

He placed a gentle finger against her lips. "You don't have to say it. You should never have had to say it, to me at least. My words that day came from a broken heart. It was a bitter day, the day I buried my father."

They scarcely heard Cici's whispered, "Excuse me," though Holly would swear later that she saw her wink as she disappeared down the hall.

"I knew I had to be wrong, but it's so much easier to say the words than to take them back. I've been trying for weeks to find a way." His hands held her shoulders, and their eyes met. "I should have trusted you. Even when I felt I couldn't trust anyone, I should have known in my heart that I could trust you. Can you forgive me?"

"I never blamed you," she told him. "But there have been so many mistakes, so many people hurt, so many betrayals."

"We could set a good example." His voice was husky. His hands dropped and held hers. "Is it too late for us to start over?"

173

Chapter Twenty

It sounds like Philip De-
LaCruz," her mother said, sur-
prised, as she handed Holly the phone a few days later.

Holly hoped Ellen didn't notice that her hand shook
as she took it. "Hello," she said tentatively.

"Hello, Holly. I, ah, I was wondering if you'd like to
have dinner with me Saturday night, and maybe go to a
movie. *Fiddler on the Roof* is playing up in San Jose."

"San Jose seems like a long way to go for a movie,"
she answered, afraid to express the joy that overwhelmed
her.

"They say it's very good, though. Of course if you'd
rather not . . ."

"Oh, no, Philip. I'd like to go, really I would."

"Really?"

"I can't think of any way I'd rather spend the evening."

"Then I'll pick you up about six—no, better make it
earlier, and we'll have dinner up there. Five thirty?"

174

"Five thirty's fine." She realized her mother was still standing in the hallway. "I'm looking forward to it."

"So am I. Good-bye until Saturday." He hung up, and Holly began counting the hours until Saturday evening.

Ellen waited. "He came to his mother's house unexpectedly while I was there last week," Holly told her. "We talked for a while. He realizes now that I had nothing to do with Julio's death. Mom, we both want to try to start over."

"Start what?"

Holly wasn't sure, herself, of the answer. "Nothing, maybe, but we were becoming good friends. All right, maybe more than friends. We just decided to see each other again, to try to pick up where we left off."

Ellen sighed. "I like Philip well enough, but he was so quick to blame you. And nothing's changed, really. Our family and his . . ."

"We're trying to reopen the investigation into Julio's death, Mother."

"And if Sam was involved, what then? Of course I hope he wasn't; it was a despicable thing to do. But he's still part of the family."

"Sam's only my second cousin," Holly protested. "And anyhow, if he had any hand in that firebombing, he should be held accountable."

"Yes, he should. But I'm afraid Philip would hold it against you. Holly, I saw your eyes light up when you answered the phone. Don't let yourself get hurt again."

"We have a date for Saturday night, to have dinner and see a movie. That's all," Holly insisted.

"Just one thing, Holly—promise me one thing.

Please take it slowly. You broke off with Greg right after you met Philip. I'm not blind; I can see how you feel about him, but you two are so different."

Holly opened her mouth to protest, but Ellen shut her off quickly. "I don't mean race, for Pete's sake. And I don't mean religion, either. I'm sure lots of those Pentecostals are good Christians. I mean your personalities. You've always been so quiet, shy, even. Philip's never going to be the kind of man who fits in, goes along. He'll fight first and think about it later. Do you want him to drag you along into his battles?"

"I'm not sure, Mom. Did I tell you he's thinking about going to South America as a missionary?"

Ellen gasped. "I thought he had a doctorate in agribusiness."

"He wants to teach modern farming and marketing techniques. There are some parachurch groups doing that sort of thing. They work with missionaries. It's not that different from what the Salvation Army's always done—feeding both body and soul, you might say."

"And what would you do in a place like that?" Ellen queried sharply.

"Heaven knows." Holly smiled at the unconscious choice of words. "Maybe heaven does know," she added. "I don't, but I do know I care deeply for Philip. And I think he brings out something good in me, some instinct for putting my good intentions into action. Who knows? Maybe my caution and his fervor are meant to complement each other."

Ellen shook her head. "There's no way I can argue with what you're saying. But I'm your mother. I have to warn you that what passes for idealism and even for love these days leads to some strange places. You're a sensible girl. Just don't get swept off your feet by a handsome man with a lot of charisma." She hesitated, uncertainly. "Like Judy," she concluded, "and Vic."

The warning wasn't lost on Holly, who had warned herself of the same thing after all. "But Philip isn't Vic. Vic's a phony. He uses causes and hides behind them. Philip is a good, decent man who fights for what he believes in."

It was nearly midnight when Philip and Holly left the theater and began the long drive back to Salinas. "It's so sad, isn't it?" Holly commented. "They had all their traditions, their steady, peaceful lives, and then, suddenly, it was all gone."

"Sad?" he questioned. "They had so much more to look forward to at the end than the beginning."

"But they were forced out of their homes, away from the only life they'd known," she said wistfully.

"So they had to change. Is it really sad that they were forced to trade the past for a future? Are memories really better than hope?"

"I guess, if you look at it that way . . ." She paused. "After all, the daughters married the men they loved, and the family went to America. But the pain . . ."

"Change does hurt, sometimes," he admitted. "But I was raised on the idea that it was good. Mama and Papa certainly never regretted leaving the Philippines."

"No, but should people be forced to change against their wills?"

"Tevye changed so his daughters could be happy. He wasn't forced."

"I didn't mean that. I meant the way they were forced out of their homes."

"God uses bad men doing bad things to bring about good sometimes. Of course that doesn't excuse the pogroms, but I still think Tevye's family came out ahead," he insisted. "And the music's superb."

Her tinkling chuckle joined his deep laugh. "No argument there." She hummed a few bars of "Sunrise, Sunset" as he slowed for the traffic signals of Gilroy and then left the town behind. "Speaking of the future, since you won't be going to South America soon, are you going to teach at Hartnell again next year?" she asked.

"I'd like to, but I was hired as a temporary replacement. I got notice last week that my contract might not be renewed."

"But I hear your students love you," she protested.

"I think I've done fairly well, for a beginner. It might just be a formality. They have to give out the notices in March, by law, or they're committed to rehire. It doesn't mean they won't offer me a job for next year—just that they don't have to."

"Oh, well, then . . ." She sighed with relief.

"I'd like to stay here another year, for Mama's sake," he went on. "But some of the college board members aren't too fond of having a Chavez supporter on their faculty."

"They can't fire you for that! What about academic freedom?"

"Who said that? Not sweet little Holly Stevens? Is my scandalous liberalism rubbing off on you?" he teased.

"I'm not *that* conservative," she protested. "You're

totally within your rights in supporting a legitimate labor organization."

"You *are* learning," he said, and she quietly basked in his approval. "But calling the UFW a legitimate labor organization isn't exactly conforming to community standards in Salinas."

She had to agree. "But it's still none of their business as long as it doesn't interfere with your teaching."

"And I may still get the new contract."

"If you don't, what will you do then?"

"Don't sound so worried," he answered. "I won't starve. In fact, I think I might get an offer from Davis. It wouldn't be bad going back there for a year or two while I wait for the Lord to work out the South America thing. Except for Mama, of course."

"Yes," she agreed. "I liked Davis. It's a good school and a nice town."

"I'm glad you think so," he whispered.

"Not that it matters what I think," she tried to cover. *Don't make a big deal of it*, she warned herself. "I just meant it would be a nice place for you to live, if you can't stay here. But Cici would like to have you nearby, for all she says she's doing fine."

"Yes, she would. If things were different—if Papa were still here and if I planned to teach for the rest of my life, Davis would be perfect. But I still believe God wants me somewhere else."

"Philip, how can you be so sure about something like that? I guess Pentecostals are different, but, well, do you hear voices or something?" She chuckled self-consciously. "We Baptists talk a lot about seeking God's will, but I always thought of it as a passive thing. You know, acceptance. How can you know what God wants you to do?"

"Wow, that is a loaded question, isn't it?" He was quiet for a while. "No, we don't hear voices," he said at last. "At least I never have. But an idea comes, and it won't go away. You pray about it. You add up the pluses and minuses. Maybe it doesn't add up logically, but the idea's still there, inside."

"But if it doesn't make sense . . . I mean, I sort of felt that way about being a med tech," she admitted. "But that was an intelligent decision, based on talent, and ability—and job prospects," she concluded.

"If all our decisions were based on logic, who'd do the pioneering, Holly?"

"Then you admit what you want to do isn't logical."

"It depends on your point of view. It may not look like the best thing, but the notion isn't totally absurd. It's something I'm trained for and have a talent for. It's something I can see purpose to—and godly purpose at that."

For him, she realized, *but not for me. It's like Mom said. What would I do there?* "You can serve God here too," she protested.

"Sure. But that isn't the point. You could probably make a good case that I would be more effective here, able to train more people even. But every time I prayed to God to show me what he wanted me to do, I just became more convinced this was it."

"Then what about the delay? Mightn't that be a sign you're wrong?"

"If it had been a definite 'no' I guess I would have taken it as that, but it wasn't. They seem committed to the program, and their plans are just what I'd been thinking of."

The lights of Salinas twinkled as they crested the hill and drove down into town. "The answer wasn't no, Holly; it was just wait a while. And it isn't hard for me to see reasons for God to delay my plans."

"Your mother?"

"That too," he said so softly she scarcely heard.

A light still burned in the living room window when he walked her to the front door. "That's funny," she remarked. "I thought Mother had finally quit waiting up for me."

"Maybe she doesn't trust me."

"Nonsense. Besides," she added, "she trusts me."

"I like that." He gripped her hand, and she treasured the warmth. "Trust is important. You can't have love without it." His eyes were glowing in the light of the porch lamp as he looked into hers, but he made no move to kiss her.

Ellen looked up as the door clicked shut. "You didn't have to wait up, Mom," Holly protested. But Ellen put a finger to her lips.

"Your father's asleep, but I just couldn't drop off. Marianne called earlier, and I thought you should know. Judy's gone. She packed her clothes and the baby's things and took off early this morning in Paul's car. She called them later to tell them she'd left the car at the bus station."

"She took the baby with her?"

Ellen nodded. "They had so hoped she'd want to stay, if only for little Carrie's sake, but her probation ended last week. Marianne was so hurt. She didn't even say good-bye to them, Holly."

"She probably couldn't face them and tell them she was going. Maybe she was afraid they'd talk her out of it."

"Or at least talk her into leaving the baby here," Ellen interrupted.

"She'd never do that. I'm sorry, Mom. I hoped Aunt Marianne would be able to get through to her. She could have, if anyone could."

"I suppose she's headed for Detroit to find that no-good Vic," Ellen sighed.

Chapter Twenty-One

April was warm and sunny that year. The hills were green from the good winter rains and golden with California poppies. Philip downshifted and guided his wheezing pickup around the tight switchbacks, and Holly dared to look down. Soledad huddled below, a tan splotch amid the rich green.

The long harvest season was already beginning. There were still scattered pickets in the Salinas Valley, but the ugly violence of last summer seemed to have worn itself out. Nationally, the Teamsters and the AFL-CIO were making peace. In the Salinas Valley a new pact between the Teamsters and the AFL-CIO-affiliated UFW gave hope to both workers and growers. While many of the independents still held out, some, like McLean-Hanlon Inc., had quietly signed with the new union.

Philip pulled into a turnout, and they looked down from their hillside perch. Below, the Salinas Valley was alive with spring. At first they reveled in the peaceful panorama, but then details began to take shape. "Look," Holly exclaimed. "Even from way up here you can tell by the colors which crop is which and what stage they're in. Some of the fields are almost solid green, where the plants are nearly full grown. Those black and green polka-dotted ones have just been thinned, I'll bet; and see the ones with the fine green lines, just sprouting?"

"Quite a sight, isn't it? Millions of dollars worth of crops, and this year everyone will have a fair share."

"Was it worth it, Philip? Did they gain enough to be worth the cost?"

"I hope so." His eyes swept the fertile valley. "It's a good beginning, if they can just follow through."

"Sometimes I wonder why you've dropped out of the union leadership. Don't they still need someone with your kind of training to keep things going in the right direction?"

"They have lots of help now." There was just a hint of bitterness in his voice. "It isn't a bunch of uneducated farm workers fighting for basic human decency anymore. Now it's officially a labor union. The AFL-CIO can give them all the professional help they need."

"Your side won, Philip, and yet you sound disappointed."

"I am, in a way. Oh, not that I'm not glad they have their union recognition, but there was something else, a cooperative spirit, a real desire to work together to make things better—the clinic, the credit union, the hiring halls. Cesar still wants that, I think, but I'm afraid they've taken his union away from him. I know they've taken it away from me."

He wheeled the car out of the turnout and farther into the hills. "It's funny, isn't it?" he commented, as they passed the sign that said "Pinnacles National Monument." "I grew up right at the foot of these hills, and this is the first time I've ever been up here."

"I was here a few times, back when I was a Girl Scout."

"That's my problem." He gave her a wry smile. "I was never a Girl Scout."

"You weren't?" She joined in his laughter. "But I thought everybody was a Scout sometime or other."

"We kids had to help on the farm a lot," he explained. "And, well, the Scouts were mostly for the other kids. I didn't take up hiking until I was a grad student at Davis."

"I've got enough badges for both of us," she assured him. "Did you bring a compass and a trail map?"

They stood close together in the spring breeze. His soft, long hair brushed her cheek as they studied the map. "It's more than 2.0 miles straight up, that way, or 1.4 miles along an old stream bed the other direction."

"I've never been over to the Balconies," she told him, "and it's probably a nice walk. But as I recall the view from the top is spectacular," she told him. "I'm game if you are."

The climb was, as promised, steep. Neither of them had breath for talking as they puffed up the switchbacks. At first the western slope was shady, but as noon approached, the spring sun came over the crest and beat down on them. Holly saw a cluster of boulders in the shadow of a live oak that leaned over the well-packed trail.

Philip, in the lead, had seen the shady nook too. "How about having lunch down here?" he suggested.

"What's the matter? You're not giving out before we get to the top, are you?" she teased. But despite her words, she sank gratefully onto one of the low stones and leaned back against the twisted oak. "It's been a while since I've done this," she admitted.

Philip ignored the basalt outcropping on the other side of the trail, settling instead onto the pebbly ground at her feet. "I might be a little out of condition," he puffed. "But I haven't given up. I just need some nourishment." He handed her the backpack he'd been carrying. "Lunch?"

She handed him a chicken sandwich. His fingers brushed hers as he took it, and she knew the touch was deliberate. Her heart was pounding, and not just from the climb. "We don't have to go all the way up."

"If you're tired . . ."

"I won't be, after we've rested a few minutes," she assured him. "We've come this far. It would be a shame not to finish."

"Yes." He opened a thermos of lemonade, filled the inner cup, and handed it to her. "I don't really understand people who climb mountains because they're there. I climb them to get to the top."

He reached for her empty cup. "Want a refill?"

"Better save some," she advised. "We're not even there yet, and I would remind you we have to come back down." She felt him watching her. "I'm saving dessert too," she explained, dropping two dark red apples back into the backpack. "I have a feeling we'll want them later."

He stood and reached down to help her up. "Okay, I'll let you set the pace the rest of the way, since you're the experienced hiker." He gave her a playful shove, and she wondered at the laughter in his voice.

She took a few steps, rounded another switchback, and ducked through a dark, damp tunnel formed by the juxtaposed jumble of red rock fragments that stood out at the top of the ridge and gave the park its name. She gasped, first, at the incredible spectacle around her, and then turned and glowered in mock anger at Philip, who grinned broadly at her. "You knew it all the time, didn't you?" she laughed. "You knew we were almost to the top."

"I peeked around the corner before I stopped," he admitted.

"And stopped! How could you?"

"I wanted a little more anticipation—like Christmas morning, when the packages are too pretty to open." He slipped one arm casually around her waist and stretched out the other, sweeping the circle of ruddy, weathered pinnacles and, between and beyond, the vista. The rounded peaks of the Gavilan range, so unlike the incongruous little patch of upheaval where Philip and Holly stood, rolled away to the north and south. The hillsides were green and poppy gold studded with amethyst spires of lupine. They lingered, hand in hand. "I feel I can see the whole world from here," Holly breathed at last.

"Do you? It's beautiful, but is the Salinas Valley really your whole world?" he asked, dropping her hands.

He cupped her face gently in his strong hands. "Is this all the world you want?"

"It's always been enough for me," she told him, knowing as she did that it wasn't the answer he wanted. "It always has been, up to now."

Voices from below interrupted their pleasure. A gaggle of teenagers clambered noisily through the tunnel and fanned out. Philip took Holly's hand, and they started back down the trail. "That's really why I stopped on the way up," he admitted when they were out of earshot. "It was crowded then, too, and I wanted it just for us."

"It has been nice, hasn't it?" she commented. "I guess most hikers come up the east side, from the visitors' center. We've had this side almost to ourselves all day."

"Could be they know enough to take the easy way." He laughed again, and reached out a hand to steady her as she maneuvered a slippery downslope. "Careful. Take it slow and easy."

His words had a familiar ring. *Almost the same words Mom used, but with such a different meaning. Still . . .* "I have a feeling that falling headlong could be painful," she said, pointing down into the boulder-strewn, mesquite-covered canyon, but thinking of Philip's arms reaching out to steady her.

They took caution, making their way slowly down the trail, pausing partway down, as Holly had suggested, to enjoy the apples in the backpack.

"I need to do this more often. I've gotten soft since I've been teaching," Philip said, as he lounged in the shade of another live oak, contemplating the last leg of the hike.

"Oh, you have?" Holly objected, as she furtively admired the ripple of his biceps. "When? While you were painting your mother's house, or on the lazy weekends when you were planting strawberries?"

"I can see Mama's been bragging. But I couldn't believe how slow I'd gotten with the berries. I could set them out twice as fast when I was in high school."

"You've been working hard." She idly stroked his browned hand. "You didn't get those calluses grading papers."

He lifted the hardened palm and covered her hand with it. "I remember something Papa said once," he mused. "The county farm adviser was telling him how to do something, and he snorted that no one without dirt under his nails could possibly teach him anything about farming." Philip casually picked a sprig of purple clover and tucked it into her hair. "Holly, I'm not going to the altiplano with soft, clean hands."

"Is it definite, then?" She dreaded the answer. "Have you heard something more?"

"We're in touch. I still don't know when, though it won't be right away." He studied her face. "I am going, Holly."

She nodded, not wanting to believe, but knowing. "Tell me about the project, Philip. All you've really said is that you'd be working with missionaries and teaching farming techniques. Would you be living in a small village or going from place to place or . . . ?"

"What we're talking about is a demonstration farm, probably near a fair-sized town. I wouldn't just be telling the people how to farm; I'd be showing them that the new ways work—fertilizers, mulches, inexpensive plastic cold-frames to lengthen the growing season. The idea is to help them help themselves, and at the same time we'll live, as well as preach, the gospel."

"You wouldn't really be going out into unexplored territory or anything like that, then?"

"What's the matter? No taste for adventure?" He reached out and brushed a caterpillar from her sleeve. "No, I'd be following the pathfinders, going where there are already established churches. This project is aimed at making earthly life better. Jesus did that—fed, healed. I just want to follow his example."

"He did it to draw people to himself, though, didn't he? Isn't that our prime responsibility as Christians?"

"Holly, I agree that the first responsibility of the church on earth is to preach the gospel, but I haven't been called as a preacher. I've been called to serve by seeing to physical needs. It's another way of preaching. If my work is done in Jesus' name, it will draw people to him too. You understand that, don't you?" The hand that covered hers pressed it tightly as he looked at her, waiting for her answer.

"I think I do, Philip. I've had a very good example in my aunt and uncle."

"Dr. and Mrs. Cameron, the Salvation Army people? Yes. How many souls do you suppose they've led to the Lord while they were ministering to people's bodies?"

He was right, she knew. *But it's his call, not mine,* she argued with herself. *I know I'm falling in love with him; I think he's falling in love with me. But if we were meant for each other, God wouldn't call one of us to a work the other can't be part of.* "I know they have found their work very satisfying," she told him. "I know they're happy."

They tucked their apple cores into Philip's backpack and retraced their steps through the chaparral-filled canyon to the car.

They were nearly back to Salinas. It had been an almost perfect day, Holly thought. *Perfect, if only there were a future in it. But his work isn't mine.*

"Cici told me the district attorney didn't feel there was enough evidence to reopen the investigation. I'm sorry." She was reluctant to inject the tragedy into the satisfyingly intimate silence, but she knew the rebuff by the "system" had reopened the wound of his father's death.

"I wasn't surprised." The tenderness that had controlled his voice up in the hills disappeared at their return to the valley's realities. "Holly, I keep telling myself they're just doing their job. There's no reason at all for them to take my word over anyone else's."

"Or vice versa?"

"It isn't that. I'm sure it isn't. If we just had some corroboration . . ."

He'd pulled up in front of the Stevenses' house. "Has there been any word from Judy since she left?"

Holly shook her head. "She's cut me off entirely. She's so sure it was me that turned them in to the sheriff."

"You?"

His obvious surprise astonished her. "Why, yes. Surely you knew that she blamed me for that. That's what drove us apart."

His low whistle puzzled her. "She blamed you for what happened at our place, Holly. I thought that was the problem. But the raid? Why should she have blamed you for that?"

"Well, it was an anonymous tip."

"I know." Now there was a hint of sardonic laughter in his low voice. "I didn't know your name was 'anonymous.'"

"I'd thought about it, Philip," she confessed. "And I talked about it once, to Aunt Marianne, at the clinic. I guess someone overheard us, and told Judy about it."

"So she blamed you. Don't those two ever talk to each other?" He was laughing openly now.

"What two?" she demanded. "What in the world is so funny?"

"It isn't really funny, Holly. It's much too serious for that. But what you don't know is that Judy's . . ." He let the phrase dangle for want of a proper word. "I always figured Vic, and so, presumably, Judy, blamed me for the raid."

"But you'd never have risked the damage to the union," she protested. "You might have ordered them out of the valley, but you'd never . . ."

"Vic doesn't really understand that kind of loyalty, Holly."

It was her turn to laugh, bitterly, remembering how often Vic had hurt Judy, abandoned her, and then turned up when he was broke and in trouble. "Him! Loyalty! How well do you know him?"

"Mostly I know about him. He managed to get in the good graces of a few of Cesar's friends," Philip explained. "He went to New York to help with the boycott—well, ostensibly to help with the boycott."

"Judy was there."

"Yes. She followed him, I gather. But he got picked up for possession. We heard about it, and kicked him off the staff."

"That would have been when they went to Detroit," Holly said.

He nodded. "According to the grapevine, he was convicted for dealing there and went to jail."

"Judy said it was for possession," Holly interrupted.

"That would have been bad enough, but, no. What I heard was that he was selling, to kids—little kids. Ten- and twelve-year-olds."

"Oh, no. Judy couldn't have known."

"I hope not. He probably told her he was framed, and she, well . . ."

"She's crazy, Philip. Maybe it's the drugs." She thought back. "No, it's him. If she hadn't been crazy over him, she'd never have started using drugs."

He looked at her, questioning. "Is that why . . . ?" he began. But he bit his lip and left the question unasked.

Holly silently finished the unspoken question. *Is that why I've been afraid to let myself fall in love with him?*

Philip was talking again about Vic. "When I recognized him on a picket line a few days before the raid, I confronted him and told him he wasn't welcome here. He made some wild accusations at the time."

"About what, for crying out loud?"

"I gathered he had a notion there was something between me and Judy. Remember, I told you I'd keep an eye on her? I drove her home a few times, tried to talk to her about the company she was keeping. I guess it could have been misinterpreted."

"He, of all people, had no right to be jealous, the way he's treated her."

"Maybe he really was trying to do right by her, Holly. There is the baby after all."

"I doubt it," Holly muttered.

Philip shrugged. "I don't understand his type, and I'm not sure I want to. But anyhow, he took a violent dislike to my telling him the UFW didn't need him. And I probably made a few threats too. I figured he was on parole, and I said something about turning him in if I saw him around again."

"How many others knew about his record?" Holly asked.

"I don't know; a few of the old-timers from Delano, probably. But I was the one who challenged him. In fact, if he hadn't been in jail when the bombing occurred, I could almost believe he had something to do with it."

"Philip, could he have known about the meeting?"

"Not likely. He wasn't a man anybody in the leadership would have trusted. And he was in jail," Philip reminded her. "How many people could he have talked to between the raid and the time they shipped him back to Michigan?"

"Judy," she said abruptly.

"Judy was sincere in her grief for my father. Whatever her problems, no matter how many mistakes she's made, she was horrified. And she'd never, never have blamed you for something she knew someone else had done—even Vic."

"Not knowingly." Holly still trusted her cousin that much. "But you don't know how thoroughly under Vic's control she is. She's always been so in love with him, so blindly in love with him."

"She's not in love with him. I don't know what it is, but that isn't love." Philip looked at Holly again with that intense, deep stare. But there was something else in his eyes—understanding, perhaps. "Love isn't blind. It's like faith: It isn't always entirely logical, but it's never blind."

They had been sitting in the car for a long time. Holly realized her mother had stepped onto the porch. "She must wonder if I'm coming in for supper, Philip. I'm sure she could set another place."

"Not today, thanks." He walked around and opened the door for her. "Maybe later."

Chapter Twenty-Two

T he weather was perfect; the flowers were glorious; we could see—forever!" Holly responded to her father's query about her day.

"And the company was good, I gather." Ellen smiled as she passed the salad bowl to her daughter. Holly was glad her mother seemed to be losing her reservations about Philip.

"We had a good talk," she told them. "About his plans, mostly."

They had just started supper. The phone rang, and Holly started for the hall. "Probably somebody trying to sell us an acre of desert," she grumbled.

The voice at the other end of the line was hoarse and halting. "Holly?" it asked. "Please don't hang up on me."

Holly didn't understand the strange request or, at first, recognize the distraught voice.

"I don't deserve your forgiveness and certainly not your help."

Judy. "Judy, is that you?"

"I'm so sorry for everything."

"I'm so glad to hear from you. Of course I'll help. What's happened?"

Judy sniffed. "I couldn't think of anyone else to call. I couldn't call Marianne after I ran out on her. I don't know anybody here, not anybody I trust, anyhow."

"Where are you?"

"I'm in Detroit. I want to come home, but the baby . . ." She sniffed again. "My baby's gone. He's taken my baby away."

"Carrie! Who took her? Vic?" Holly tried to piece the fragments together. "Judy, slow down and tell me what's happened."

"Vic—oh, Holly, you wouldn't believe what he's been doing. When I found out, I left him. But now he's taken Carrie."

"Have you gone to the police?"

"They took a report, but they don't really care. We're just a couple of hippies as far as they're concerned. I can't find him."

"Would he hurt Carrie?"

"He might do anything. He's—you couldn't imagine. Drugs, and dealing, and . . ." Judy paused, and continued a little less hysterically. "Holly, I have to find her and bring her home."

"Tell me exactly where you are. I'll be there as soon as I can catch a plane."

"I hate to ask, after the way I've hurt you. I wouldn't, for me, but I'm so afraid for Carrie."

Holly's plane arrived Sunday evening. It wasn't spring yet in Detroit. She shivered in her light raincoat as the wind drove melting snow against her face. She felt terribly alone in the vast airport terminal. *Maybe I should have taken Dad up on his offer to come with me,* she thought.

The cab driver's eyebrows knit into a menacing frown when she gave him the address. "You sure that's the right place, young lady?" he questioned.

"Yes," she answered nervously. "That's where I'm to meet my cousin."

"It's a pretty rough neighborhood," he muttered. "You don't look like the type to be going there." His voice dropped to a stage whisper. "But I guess you never can tell." Louder he warned her. "I'll take you, but I won't wait, not there."

Even with the cab driver's warning, Holly was unprepared for the decrepit street. Ugly stumps between broken sidewalk and littered street proved there had once been trees. Once dignified two-story homes with wide porches crouched in weedy, trampled yards that used to be lawns. Half of the downstairs windows were boarded up; the other half barred.

Despite the driver's words, the cab hadn't pulled away from the curb after she paid him. *He is waiting.* She was grateful. *There must be some mistake. But this house looks better than most on the block,* she told herself. *At least the beer cans have been picked up. But what if Judy isn't here?*

A woman answered Holly's timid knock—a grandmotherly woman with steel gray hair pulled firmly into a bun, wearing a well-worn, old-fashioned house dress, starched and pressed. *Here, amidst this squalor.* The butterflies in Holly's stomach quieted even before the woman smiled in answer to her inquiry. *Her appearance must have reassured the cab driver too*, Holly thought, as she heard him drive off.

"Judy's room is the second on the left, upstairs. You must be the cousin she said was coming. I'm so glad to see you."

Judy wore jeans and a tank top, but they were clean. Her carrot-red hair was pulled back into a neat ponytail. Her room was neat, too, Holly realized when the two had finally finished hugging each other, Judy tearfully begging forgiveness and Holly, equally tearful, assuring her of it. "I was afraid I had the wrong place," she told Judy as she looked around.

Judy nodded. "The neighborhood's pretty awful. Vic was out of prison and living down the street when I got here. I didn't know where else to go, after . . . Mrs. O'Day's an angel," she concluded.

"That's what I thought when she opened the door," Holly said. "What is this place? A rooming house?"

"Technically, I guess it's just a rooming house. But Mrs. O'Day calls it her 'mission.' She's lived here for decades, since this was one of the 'better' neighborhoods. After her husband died, she thought of moving away, but then property values dropped, and she didn't have much money. So she just stayed on, renting out a few rooms to make ends meet. And picking up 'strays.'"

Holly's eyes followed Judy's around the little room. The furniture was Grand Rapids circa 1940—scratched and chipped, but polished to a sheen. Chintz curtains hung at the single window. A patchwork quilt covered the bed, and a second, smaller one was folded in the empty crib.

"You haven't had any news about the baby, have you?" Holly asked.

Judy shook her head, and tears slipped down her cheeks.

"Maybe you should try to start at the beginning." Holly sat on the bed next to her and slipped an arm around her shoulder. "You found Vic here and were living with him?"

Judy sniffed back her sobs. "He was back on the stuff as soon as he got out of jail. I was clean, Holly. I stopped using after the raid because I realized that if I were ever picked up again, they'd take Carrie away from me. But he didn't care. He wouldn't even try."

Judy's eyes drifted back to the empty crib. "He was dealing, too, and to kids. I kept thinking I could change him," she said. "I loved him. But he was using drugs, hard stuff even, and dealing. And then I found out he was . . ."

She stared down at her hands. "He was using girls—young girls, thirteen, fourteen years old. He'd give them speed or coke and get them hooked. Then, when they didn't have money to buy more stuff he'd . . . well, he'd help them get it."

"Stealing?" Holly asked.

"Worse."

Holly shuddered. "Prostitution?"

Judy's face confirmed Holly's guess without words. "We had an awful fight. I told him I was leaving. He laughed at me, told me he could always find somebody to pay his rent and share his bed—somebody younger and fresher than me. That was the night he told me about the bombing."

"The bombing? At the DeLaCruzes'?" Holly interrupted. "What did he tell you?"

"I think he told me to scare me, to let me know just what he was capable of. I feel so terrible about it. He had told me, when he was in jail in Salinas, that you told my father about the meeting. But it was him."

"But how?" Holly recalled Philip's suspicions. "How, if he was in jail?"

"He was cooperative, you might say, with one of the deputies who'd been particularly tough on the pickets. Vic had overheard someone talking about the union meeting, so he passed the word along."

"A deputy sheriff? Philip told me he recognized one of the men, but the sheriff's office didn't do anything."

"No wonder. Anyhow, Vic 'suggested' to this deputy that the farmers' association would probably be 'grateful' if someone ran Chavez out and that he should talk to my father."

"I know Sam was furious, but I never believed he was actually involved, Judy."

"Vic planned it all. He blamed Philip for the raid, and he wanted to get back at him, so he sent the man to my father. The man offered to scare Cesar off, for money. I don't think any of them, except Vic, maybe, intended to kill anyone, but . . ." She shuddered. "It was all my fault."

Holly's eyes brimmed and overflowed. "Judy, it's over now. The important thing is to find Carrie and get you both back home."

"I want that so much," Judy sighed. "But I don't know what more I can do to find her."

"You said Vic took her."

"After he told me everything, I left him. Mrs. O'Day let me come here—she wouldn't have him; she doesn't take users. But she knew I was clean, so she let me move in with Carrie. I got a job waiting tables, and one of the other girls who lives here was watching Carrie. Vic came and said he was supposed to bring Carrie to me at work, and she let him have her. That was a week ago."

"What have you done so far? You said the police took a report, but I gather you haven't heard anything from them."

"He's her father, Holly. I guess the police think that makes it all right."

"With his record?"

"He isn't wanted for anything at the moment. Oh, I gave them some names and addresses, but they've got bigger things to worry about than scum like him, I guess. I've been on the streets, asking about her. I've gone to the people he hangs out with, but nobody will tell me anything. And I've been praying," she added softly. "Holly, surely Jesus won't let anything happen to my baby, no matter what I've done."

Holly squeezed her cold hand. "Judy, have you come back to him?" she asked.

"I'm trying." Judy lifted her tear-stained face. "I've gone so far, hurt him so. I know God promised to forgive, but I've broken every commandment short of murder."

"He loves you, just like I love you, and your father loves you—only more."

"Mrs. O'Day reminded me a few days ago about the woman taken in adultery—I called Vic my husband but I guess she knew better. 'Go,' Jesus told her, 'and sin no more.' But I knew Jesus, once, and I turned my back on him."

"You can't undo what you've done, I guess, and you can't gloss it over either. But Jesus did die to save sinners."

"'To seek and to save that which was lost,'" Judy quoted. "I memorized that verse because it was short." She laughed ruefully. "Short, but very sweet. I do believe it, Holly, but it's so hard to really believe in that kind of love."

Holly prayed with Judy, for faith and for help in their search. Then they tried to sleep. The next morning they went, together, to the police station.

"Bigelow?" the desk sergeant repeated brusquely. "That name's familiar." He ran a finger down a list in a desk drawer and frowned. He disappeared before they could say anything and came back with a smudged manila folder in his hand.

"I don't quite know how to tell you this, except to come out and say it, ladies. We found a Vic Bigelow three days ago—overdose."

Judy didn't speak. Her face showed no emotion.

"Is he in a hospital?" Holly asked.

The sergeant shook his head. "Dead when he was found," he answered. "I'm sorry."

Judy gasped, and the sergeant's face softened. "Hey," he said, his voice less gruff now, "I wish I had better news." He studied the contents of the folder. "Says here that his parents in San Francisco were notified. They declined to claim the body, so . . ."

He looked at Judy and his face became almost kind.

"I can arrange for you to claim the ashes, if you want to make any arrangements . . ."

"Sergeant, I thought, once, that I loved him," Judy sighed. "He fathered my child, and I love her. But it was too late for me to do anything for Vic a long time ago."

Despite the calmly measured words, Holly read despair on her cousin's face. "He took my baby from me last week. There's a little girl out there. She's less than a year old," she said. "We've got to find her."

"We will," the desk sergeant vowed. "I've got a granddaughter that age." He picked up a pen. "Give me everything you can—a picture, a description of what she was wearing, friends he might have left her with."

Though he tried to be reassuring, both young women left the station with heavy hearts. Somewhere in the strange, cold city, a baby not quite a year old was lost. "I don't know which would be worse," Judy sobbed. "Alone and hungry or with some of those, those . . ." She shuddered. "Holly, if she cried they might give her something to keep her quiet."

"A baby." Holly tried to reassure her. "Everyone loves babies."

"Suppose we never find her. Suppose she dies all alone out there, or suppose she grows up in one of those houses, with somebody like her father."

"The police are going to search for her, Judy. They'll find her." Holly wished she believed her own words.

It was the uniform that first caught Holly's eye. The woman was dressed in a dark navy suit with the familiar red "S" on the collar. She was tall and gray-haired and walked with the same purposeful stride Aunt Marianne did. She climbed the steps of an old brownstone in better repair than those around it, and Holly saw the sign on the door.

"It's a Salvation Army shelter, Judy," she said. "Why don't we go in?"

"What can they do?" Judy sighed. "Even if someone did bring Carrie here, they'd just call the police, wouldn't they?"

"I guess so. But sometimes people tell them things they wouldn't tell the police. And at least someone will pray with us."

A vase of pussy willow, forced into early bloom, sat on a table in the entrance hall. A door to the left stood slightly ajar, and Holly heard voices—one steady, asking questions, and the other high-pitched, frenzied. Holly sat on a bench next to the door and pulled Judy down beside her.

"Let's go back to Mrs. O'Day's," Judy protested. "The police might call."

"I just feel like we should wait here," Holly insisted. "I can't explain it. Maybe it's just because the woman I saw coming in reminded me of Aunt Marianne," she chuckled. "Or maybe it's all the old family history about the Salvation Army always being there whenever the McLeans really need help."

The door opened. A thin, hollow-cheeked girl in a black miniskirt and too-tight sweater paused in the doorway. The steady voice was still speaking. "Are you sure you don't want to stay with us for a few days? You're more than welcome here, you know."

The girl in the doorway responded shrilly. "I'm okay. It's just that I didn't know what to do with the kid. He never came back for her. You won't tell anybody about me, will you?" she pleaded. "If he ever finds out I brought the kid here, he'll kill me, sure, but I can't keep taking care of her forever. And I can't go to the cops, you know."

Holly held her breath. *It isn't exactly that I don't believe in miracles*, she insisted to herself, *but this is the twentieth century. God doesn't work that way anymore, does he?*

Judy must have heard too. She took Holly's hand and gripped it so tightly that Holly's fingers ached.

The girl slipped out furtively, still afraid of being seen. "She looks vaguely familiar," Judy whispered. "Oh, Holly, could it be?" She stood, started for the door, then drew back. "You go in. I'm afraid to."

Holly knocked softly on the half-open door, and a hand reached out. "I'll be with you in just a few minutes." The door opened the rest of the way, and a Salvation Army officer came out with a red-headed toddler in her arms. "We have a bit of an emergency here," she began.

Judy's shout of joy and Carrie's gleeful "Mama" cut her short.

She looked from child to mother, questioning for an instant. Then she placed Carrie in Judy's outstretched arms and invited them into her office. Judy was too overwhelmed to say much, so Holly repeated the story first for the smiling Salvation Army soldier and then for the police officer who came to investigate.

They spent one more night with a delighted Mrs. O'Day, who could only repeat, over and over, "Praise the Lord."

"Now I know he has forgiven me," Judy told them both. "He's forgiven me, and I promise I will love him and trust him all my life, and I'll raise Carrie to love him too."

Chapter Twenty-Three

Judy had to go to her father alone. Holly prayed with her for the faith she needed to face him and confess her own fault and for God's preparation of Sam's heart too. Holly told her parents only that Vic was dead and that Judy had returned to the Lord and needed their help to turn her life around.

"So it's all broken wide open," Philip told Holly several days later, over dinner at the Restaurante Manila. "The deputy I saw that night has been arrested for arson and voluntary manslaughter."

"Because of what Judy told the sheriff? I was afraid that wouldn't be enough."

"It wasn't, by itself. Holly, Sam McLean's come forward."

Holly gasped.

Philip's fingers circled her wrist gently. "I'm sorry," he told her. "I kept hoping he really wasn't involved. He said some awful things back then, but, well, so did a lot of other people."

"Your father's death shocked him terribly. He changed after that. Philip, I know it was an awful thing he did, but will he have to go to prison? Now? When he and Judy have another chance?"

"That's why the district attorney talked to Mama and me about it. It seems what he paid them to do—two of those thugs on the Teamster payroll were in the car too—was to interrupt the meeting, make a lot of noise and some threats. They never discussed tactics. Sam said so, and the deputy, once he knew he was trapped, corroborated his story. He insists the bomb was the Teamster goons' idea."

"It was a conspiracy, and a man died, but Philip, what would it accomplish to put him on trial and ruin what's left of his life?"

"A trial might scare some sense into some of the others, Holly." Philip absently offered her the last of the lumpia. "But the event itself did a lot of that. The D.A. is willing to let him plead no contest to a conspiracy charge and take a suspended sentence, if Mama and I agree."

She nibbled at the pastry and waited. Holly knew Philip, and she knew Cici. There was no need for her to plead for mercy.

"I went to talk to Sam. He's a broken man. He's paid for what he did every day since it happened. He begged me, in tears, to forgive him. Not that I wouldn't press charges, Holly, but that I would forgive him."

"It's a hard thing."

"Too hard for me, on my own. But he's asked God's forgiveness. He's my Christian brother. We prayed together, the three of us—he and Judy and I. The healing will take a while, but it's begun."

"I knew that would be your decision," she whispered. "It's right."

They left the restaurant hand in hand. "Would you like to take in a movie?" Philip asked without enthusiasm. "Or maybe take a drive up into the hills?"

She shook her head. "I think I should go home, Philip. At a time like this, I should be with the family."

"Sure." There was disappointment in his assent but understanding too. "This will be hard on the McLean clan. Family's important."

Family was important, to both of them. That was why Holly was so happy when her father suggested inviting Cici and Philip to Sunday dinner. Her mother agreed, and Holly was delighted when Philip accepted. "Of course we'll come," he told her. "I already like your parents, and I know Mama will too," he assured her. "They produced you, didn't they?"

"I know it's kind of old-fashioned," Holly apologized. "But they've always had this thing about knowing all my friends' families. Of course they've already met you, and it sounds rather overprotective, but they do mean well."

"I'm glad they're protective. My folks were the same way, and I intend to know my kids' friends, too, one of these days," he assured her.

"Just so you understand it doesn't mean anything, like . . ."

He laughed, and she laughed with him. She laughed more easily every time they were together, Holly realized. *Whatever happened to the tingly, trembly excitement I used to feel whenever I saw him?* she wondered. *I was afraid of falling in love with him wasn't I? But I'm not afraid anymore.*

She still warmed to the caress of his look; still shivered at the vibrato of his low voice; still hungered for the casual touch of his hand. But she was comfortable with him, too, enjoying the silences, revelling in the easy laughter, trusting herself. *What was it he had said about a rosebud needing warmth to open?*

"I promise I'll be on my best behavior and make a good impression." He crossed his heart, and they both laughed again at the childish gesture. "And I'll warn Mama not to be too obvious with her matchmaking."

"So you're wise to her too."

The laughter came again, but when he spoke it was with the intense sincerity that had become so familiar. "Holly, you know you've made us both love you. If only everything were that simple."

They gathered in the Stevenses' dining room. *Two days ago I was telling myself how comfortable I've become with Philip,* Holly recalled, *and dear Cici, warm, open Cici, with her anything-but-subtle matchmaking. Mom and Dad don't usually dabble in small talk, either. So how come we're sitting here around the table talking about the weather?*

"Holly's tried out some of your recipes on us," Ellen offered. "It's an interesting cuisine, the way it combines Oriental and Spanish influences. It looks like a lot of work, though."

Cici nodded. "But so is American food when it is done right." Her moon face forced its half-moon smile as she cut a bite of Ellen's tender pot roast. "I have never learned how to roast beef so that it is tender and moist like this."

Silence fell again, and Ron made a stab. "The lettuce crop looks big this year. Do you think prices will hold up well?"

"Well enough, sir," Philip answered, a little too respectfully. He hesitated, glanced at Holly, and decided to continue. "For union lettuce, that is. The boycott isn't over."

Cici and Ellen both drew quick breaths, but Ron seemed pleased by Philip's honest answer. "I think it is over, for all practical purposes, Phil—because there isn't that much nonunion lettuce left. You won."

"Not me, Mr. Stevens. The workers. At least I hope so."

"Then you have some doubts too. I wondered."

"It's a step forward. Just having the union gives them a chance. But it isn't the whole answer."

"Holly says you're not working with them anymore. I'm sorry to hear that." All three of the women stared as Ron continued. "They need steady leadership to maintain their gains. But, of course, after what happened to your family, I can understand your reaction." Ron looked from Philip to Holly. "I would like to have fought my own board's action last summer, but when you have a family to consider . . ."

"Philip didn't leave the union because of what happened to his father," Cici interrupted. "He wasn't frightened off."

"Mama." Philip laid a gentle hand on his mother's arm. "Mr. Stevens, my mother's right. I left because my work there was finished. I met Cesar Chavez when I was doing my doctoral research. I believed, and still believe, in his cause, but it isn't my life's work."

"You'll be concentrating on your teaching position, then," Ellen said hopefully.

"For the next several weeks anyhow," he told her. "Actually, my job at Hartnell is temporary too. I hope to be going to South America within a year."

Deep frown lines formed in Ellen's forehead. "Holly said something about that possibility, but I didn't realize it was settled."

"I don't quite understand what you would do there," Ron said, looking from Philip to Holly and back again.

Holly shifted uneasily. "Philip feels God has called him to do missionary work."

"I wasn't aware you had seminary training," Ron pressed.

"I don't. I'd be teaching farming." The fire burned in Philip's eyes. "It's a parachurch project working in established mission fields, teaching modern agricultural methods, organizing producer co-ops, putting Christianity into action."

"Well, that certainly sounds—challenging would be the right word, I guess." Ellen's words were directed to Philip, but her eyes were on her daughter.

Ron, too, stared at Holly, whose own eyes were fixed on Philip's animated face. "That would be a fine thing to do for a few years," he said tentatively. "For a young man with nothing to tie him down."

Ellen broke an uneasy silence. "We spent several years overseas when Holly was little, you know."

"Yes, I was a civil engineer and worked with the

Marshall Plan for a while in Europe. I was with a company that built canneries, commercial freezers, things like that," Ron explained. "Then I got the offer to manage the packing house here."

"Holly was about ten years old by then." Holly tried to concentrate on her dinner plate as her mother spoke. "And she'd gone to half a dozen schools already. She was such a shy little thing. We wanted her to have more stability in her life."

"You never mentioned that, Holly," Philip said. "I had the idea you'd never been out of the Salinas Valley except for college."

"I was little then. I . . ." She toyed with the mashed potatoes and gravy on her plate. "This has always been home." Her eyes met Philip's across the table and saw disappointment in them. "I've always been happy here."

The small talk resumed; the table was cleared; Ellen insisted she'd do the dishes "later"; and the evening staggered to an end.

For a few days he didn't call. Holly felt empty. *I know how he feels about the South America project,* she pondered. *And it's wrong of me to want him to give it up. It's God's will for him. But what use would I be there? I can't preach; I've no gift for teaching even.*

She put a stack of culture plates back in the incubator and walked over to the sink where a few stool specimens awaited her attention. Holly was rotating through the microbiology department in the hospital lab—not a popular assignment, but somebody had to do it.

She went through the messy, tedious steps of preparation, then slipped a freshly stained slide under her microscope. *Another negative, no doubt,* she grumbled. *I wouldn't mind doing parasitology if I ever found anything.*

Her hand, on the screw that moved the slide back and forth on the microscope stage, stopped, turned half a turn back and stopped again. Little eye-like nuclei looked back at her from a cyst, standing out like black beacons in the sea of blue hues. She counted them. *Four.* She focused up and down. *Definitely four.* She marked the spot and resumed her scanning, excited, now. *Yes, there's another one. Four nuclei and a smooth chromatoidal bar.*

She found only two of the telltale cysts. She called Tom. "I think I've got something," she told him.

He squinted, focused on the spot she'd marked, and shook his head. "I don't know how you spotted it, but I think you're right. It sure looks like a histolytica. I can't remember when we've actually found a pathogen in a stool."

Holly left the smear under the microscope. All the other techs drifted back to peek at the rare, in Salinas, amoebic parasite. "Mexican?" someone asked.

"Probably. The name's Gonzales," Holly shrugged. "He probably went home for the off-season and brought it back with him," she theorized. "I guess there are places down there where almost everybody has a parasite or three."

"Well I'd never have noticed it," Kathy offered. "Tom said you only found two cysts. Hey, wasn't it you that found the malaria last month too? You must have a gift for spotting bugs."

"I just got lucky," she protested.

"Lucky for the patient," Kathy retorted. "A few pills and, voilà, no more tummy ache."

No more tummy ache. Holly felt, again, the sense of worth, of value, that came with a difficult diagnosis, especially one that was followed by a good prognosis. *And no more anemia from the chronic intestinal bleeding either.* It felt good to make a life longer and better.

She mentioned the feeling to Cici at lunch. "It's why I became a tech," she told her friend. "So often the interesting things we find are bad news, but when it's something like this, something that can be treated easily . . ."

"Kathy said you had a gift, Holly."

"Oh, I don't think it's anything special. She'd probably have spotted them too. I mean, they were right there, staring," she chuckled, "almost winking, at me."

"It's been a good day," she told her mother that evening. "I like it when I've accomplished something."

It was an even better evening because Philip called. "I hope you can go to church with me Sunday evening," he told her. "There's going to be a guest speaker, and I especially want you to hear him."

"Who is it?"

"I'd like that to be a surprise. If you'll come, I promise you won't be disappointed."

Chapter Twenty-Four

She was surprised, but not disappointed. Dr. Hanson was from the parachurch group planning Philip's project in the altiplano. He was a lean, balding man with a small, slightly crooked nose and thin, pale lips. But his eyes, though pale gray, glowed just as Philip's black ones did when he talked of the project they were planning.

"... as most of you know, since one of your own will be going out early next year to take charge of that phase of our program." *Early next year.* She glanced at Philip, and he nodded.

He had taken her hand as they sat together, listening to Dr. Hanson's plans for the demonstration farm. Now, as he proceeded to the next point in his presentation, Philip's hand gripped hers more tightly.

"... poor nutrition, contaminated water, parasitic diseases that sap their strength and rob them of the will to better themselves."

Holly's ears perked. Her attention riveted on what

was being said, even as she felt Philip's hand tremble. "We are praying," the speaker continued, "that God will send us a doctor or someone with some medical background. If we could only test the water for safety, and treat the more common infections . . ."

Philip was too wise to comment on Dr. Hanson's words as he drove Holly home. *Someone who knew what the infections were, who could determine which drug to give when, who had the skill and training to tell them which water sources to use and when water must be boiled first. Do I have a gift?* Holly wondered, for the first time in her life. She looked to Philip for an answer, but he kept his eyes on the road. She had to decide this alone. *Could I really be useful there, by his side—not just in the way?*

"You?" Ellen protested, a few days later, when Holly confided to her mother the idea that she might, indeed, go to South America with Philip.

"If he asks me, that is."

"If he loved you, he'd never ask that of you," Ellen insisted. "He'd understand how hard it would be for you. Holly, honey, you've always hated new places, new people. It was such a struggle for you even to go away to college. If Greg hadn't been at Davis . . ."

"If Greg hadn't been at Davis I might have gone somewhere else. But he was, so I took the easy way. I knew I had to go to Oakland for my training, and I did. It was hard, at first, but I made it. And I'd have gotten a job on my own too. But Dad put in a good word with Tom, so I took the easy way out again."

Ellen was staring at her. "Of course we helped. That's what parents are for."

Holly didn't want to hurt her mother. She treasured the close, loving home she'd been raised in. "I know, but I'm grown up now. Philip . . ." *That's why he hasn't asked me yet to marry him.* She understood, at last. *Philip will never tell me what to do. He wants me to stand on my own.* "Mom, it's not an easy choice, and I won't make it lightly, but I felt I should warn you that I am thinking about it."

"You do that, Holly. You think about it, carefully. Philip is a very attractive young man. Are you sure you're not being carried away by his romantic notions?"

"I love him, Mom." It was the first time she had actually admitted it out loud. "I know I 'fell in love' with him the first time I saw him, and that isn't what love is all about. But I know him now, and the more I know him the more I love him. That's real."

Ellen laid aside the mending she'd been doing. "Yes," she sighed. "I've seen it growing. But if he feels the same way, and if it is God's will for you to marry, surely he'll see that this other idea is completely foolhardy."

"But why? You believe God calls people to be missionaries. You give money to missions faithfully. You must know someone's son or daughter uses that money."

"You're not right for it. You're shy; you get positively ill at the thought of making a speech. And you're not that strong physically, either. You've always caught everything that came along: measles, mumps, colds."

"No more than any kid, Mom. And look at it this way. I've had them all; I'm immune," she insisted with a grin.

"You hate traveling, new places, new . . ."

"Do I? Sure, I hated starting new schools when I was little and the other kids laughed at me because I didn't know the local customs. But I can learn. I always learned."

"What about your job? You're so good at it, and you always wanted a career."

"I'd have my career there too," she insisted. "I'd be using my training more there than I do here. Why shouldn't my becoming a med tech and my falling in love with Philip both be God's leading? Why shouldn't the South America project be as much my purpose in life as his?"

"Are you trying to convince me," Ellen asked, "or yourself?"

Ellen was very close to the truth, Holly realized. The more she tried to persuade her mother, the more she persuaded herself. *Philip said God revealed his will as an idea that wouldn't go away. And it does make sense, even if it's not the sense my mother sees. I have been prepared for it.*

"Maybe both," Holly admitted. "It isn't an easy decision for me. Philip is absolutely sure God wants him in South America. I'm not sure, not yet, that he wants me there too."

"But you will be sure, if Philip asks you to marry him, won't you? Your father . . ." Ellen looked away, and then back to her daughter. "Your father loved God, always, and I, well, let's say I had some problems with my faith in my youth. It kept us apart for several years."

Holly knew the story. "Dad knew he couldn't force his faith on you. You're strong. You always were. But I'm not. I do take the easy way when I can, and Philip knows that. He could force his call on me. I think he knows I'd say yes if he asked. But he won't ask unless he knows I'm ready."

Spring passed quickly. Holly and Philip spent most Saturdays together, hiking in the golden hills or strolling beside the pounding surf. He took her to supper at least once a week.

They had slipped into an easy pattern of spending Sunday evenings together, worshiping one week at her church amid the sideways glances of her old friends, and the next at his chapel, where she was learning to lift holy hands and sway with the rest of the congregation to the rhythm of the gospel music they both loved.

She waited for his question, yet dreaded it, still not certain of her answer.

In early June, Kathy and Greg were married at the Baptist church where Holly had assumed, once, that she would marry him. Instead, she stood beside Kathy. The old "always a bridesmaid, never a bride" had flashed through her mind as she preceded Kathy down the aisle, but then she saw Philip seated with his mother among the lab people who constituted most of the bride's friends.

No doubt she should have been listening to Pastor Bishop's sermon, *but what young woman does, at a wedding?* Holly smiled to herself as she imagined another scene not far in the future. *My future?* The church would be packed, no doubt, with all the Stevenses and Hanlons and McLeans packed into the bride's side, and all the DeLaCruzes, and their friends, and Philip's college colleagues filling the opposite pews. *And his UFW friends. That would make for a lively reception.* The thought broadened her smile. *I wonder if we dare invite Chavez.*

Of course, he hasn't asked me yet, she was forced to remind herself. *His job? His contract wasn't renewed, but is he so old-fashioned that he won't propose because he doesn't have a regular paycheck at the moment? He's running his mother's farm, after all. And by the time the farm is sold, he'll be going to South America.*

Will I go with him? Can I possibly let him go without me?

The pastor was closing with prayer for the newlyweds. Holly prayed, too, and listened, and knew the answer. *Lord, you do want me to go with him, don't you?*

The sun was dipping into the Pacific. After the wedding, Holly had changed to a softly flaring A-line sheath of apple-green crepe. Philip had removed his suit jacket and unaccustomed tie as soon as they left the wedding reception. Now, as they lingered over supper at a fine restaurant on the Big Sur coast, Holly was struck, again, by the way the open-necked, short-sleeved white shirt set off the deep bronze of his throat and arms.

"It's obvious why this place is world famous," she said idly. "Even if the food weren't out of this world, who'd care, with a view like this." But her eyes were on Philip's brooding face. He wasn't looking at the sunset, either. She felt the flush of her cheeks as he took her hands across the table. "Mama's had an offer for the farm."

She drew a sharp breath. "So soon?"

"They want to take over in sixty days. It's good, for her. She'll have enough cash to buy a decent place in town and still help Angie and John through college."

"And you?" She strained to hear his answer over the thumping of her heart. "What will you do?"

"Well, for the next sixty days I'll be growing strawberries. After that . . ." His eyes seemed to be searching hers, looking for something deep in them. "Holly, that's for you to tell me."

"You always said you knew what God wanted you to do, Philip. Has something changed?"

"I can still go to South America. They still want me, but . . ." His voice was husky. His hands, still holding hers, were damp. "I'm not sure anymore, Holly. What I am sure of is that I can't imagine a future without you."

He lifted one of her hands in both of his, stroking her fingers tenderly as he spoke. "I couldn't ask you to marry me when my dream seemed so wrong for you."

"It isn't, you know. My dream is to be beside you."

It was as if he hadn't heard her. "I have a firm offer from Davis now. It's an assistant professorship, in agribusiness—labor relations. With the changes in the law, it's a whole new field and an exciting one. If I took it, you would go with me, wouldn't you?"

"You would do that, for me?"

He nodded, but the coals that were his eyes seemed to have lost some of their glow. "I love you. And I believe God is in that love. The other . . ." He looked on the sea, glistening with the last reflected gold of the setting sun. "Maybe I was wrong. Davis is the right place for you, so maybe it is for me too."

Her fingers entwined with his, caressing the proud calluses. There was no doubt left in her heart. "You weren't wrong about your calling, Philip. I am as sure as you ever were that God wants you to go to South America."

"Holly!" An almost frightened gasp escaped his taut lips. "I can't drag you there. And I can't go alone."

"Just you try going alone!" she warned. "Philip, God wants both of us to go." She saw the fire come back to his eyes as he took in her words. "I want to go with you. I want to be with you, always. And I can be of use too. I even seem to have a bit of a gift for parasitology."

"I know," he whispered. "I watched you at work in the clinic last summer, and I thought how well we could work together. But then Papa . . ."

"That's over."

"The thing about Papa is over, but it was never the real issue between us. God had given me a call he hadn't given you. I love you, Holly, but strong as my love is, is it enough to sustain you in a place like that, with all its hardships?"

"I loved you the first moment I laid eyes on you," Holly assured him. "The months after your father died were terrible for me, without you. Wherever God sends you, he sends me," she vowed.

"Davis would be so much easier. And when we have children—well, if . . ."

"When," she said firmly. "When we have children, we will trust God for them too. Sure, teaching at Davis would be easier, for both of us. But it wouldn't be right."

"For you?" he queried, uncertain still. "I can't take you to the altiplano unless it's right for both of us." One of his hands still rested on hers, but the other cupped her chin. He leaned across the intimate table for two, and his lips brushed hers.

"It is," she whispered.

About the Author

Jean Grant was born in Michigan but has lived most of her life in northern California. She earned her bachelor's degree from the University of California at Berkeley and has worked for more than thirty years as a clinical laboratory technologist.

Grant's first novel was *The Revelation*. Her articles and short stories have appeared in such publications as *Evangelical Beacon*, *Mature Living*, *Home Life*, *Seek*, and *Power for Living*. *The Promise of the Harvest* is the fourth book in the Salinas Valley Saga. It is preceded by *The Promise of the Willows*, *The Promise of Peace*, and *The Promise of Victory*.

❧